Ecstasy Romance®

EVERY INCH OF HER BODY PALPITATED TO THE BEAT OF HIS HEART SO NEAR HER OWN. . .

There was a long moment of awkward silence while they listened to the shallow rhythm of their breathing as it slowly eased into normalcy.

"I want to be your friend," he whispered.

"And do you always kiss your friends that way?"

"That kiss had nothing to do with our friendship."

"And just what did it have to do with?" Chris asked, her voice rising boldly.

Warren's masterful gaze captured her face, her attention, and her will. "I think you know the answer to that question yourself." The echo of his richly vibrating words plunged into the deepest part of her, stirring the most elemental embers of her physical being into a flame of desire.

A CANDLELIGHT ECSTASY ROMANCE ®

PASSIONATE APPEAL

Elise Randolph

A CANDLELIGHT ECSTASY ROMANCE®

Dedicated to my father—
All those early years sitting at the dinner table on Black's
Law Dictionary must have made some sort of impression.

To Our Readers:

We have been delighted with your enthusiastic response to Candlelight Ecstasy Romances®, and we thank you for the interest you have shown in this exciting series.

In the upcoming months we will continue to present the distinctive sensuous love stories you have come to expect only from Ecstasy. We look forward to bringing you many more books from your favorite authors and also the very finest work from new authors of contemporary romantic fiction.

As always, we are striving to present the unique, absorbing love stories that you enjoy most—books that are more than ordinary romance. Your suggestions and comments are always welcome. Please write to us at the address below.

Sincerely,

The Editors
Candlelight Romances
1 Dag Hammarskjold Plaza
New York, New York 10017

CHAPTER 1

Two obstinate pairs of eyes glared at each other across the judge's bench. Chris's were steel-gray and idealistically determined. Those of the Honorable Judge Pierce were an older, equally determined, yet less patient brown.

Ignoring the fact that without her glasses Chris was seeing only a vague, shadowy outline of the adjudicator, she continued to lash out in self-righteous indignation.

"Your Honor, there is absolutely no excuse for this proceeding to be delayed any longer. This is the third time opposing counsel has been granted a postponement, and I must protest. It's also the third time that chief counsel for the defense has moved for a continuance without even appearing here in person."

The slim but expressive hands that had been abetting her in this demonstration of outrage now rested on her waist in a self-assured posture.

The attorney standing next to her before the judge's bench cleared his throat. "I'm the ad-interim counsel in this matter, Ms. Davis." The young man who had had the misfortune to come up against Chris shifted nervously on his feet and was beginning to break out in a cold sweat under the onslaught of her frozen scowl. The look she was giving him relegated him to nothing more than imbecile status. He had heard about this inflexible, intense female attorney from the D.A.'s office and, yes, he had been warned about her temper, but he never expected her to be half as formidable an opponent as she turned out to be. After all, for heaven's sake, she was only a woman.

"I realize," Chris tilted her head in disdain, "that the eminent Warren J. Hamilton stocks a supply of errand boys to run his—"

"Young lady!" The judge's voice finally snapped loose from the constraints of his patience at the same moment his gavel fell with a resounding thud to the wooden desk. "I will not have disparaging or derogatory comments about opposing counsel uttered in my courtroom. Is that clear?"

Swallowing another imaginative retort, Chris grudgingly nodded acquiescence.

"Now, I will repeat once more for the benefit of the prosecuting attorney . . ." He peered over his rimless spectacles at Chris. "This case is postponed until two weeks from today, August fifth, eleven A.M." He dropped the gavel to the desk one more time for effect, then rose stiffly and stepped down from the bench.

Chris watched the hazy receding figure until the door to his chambers had snapped shut. She whirled back around to face her opponent, ready to lambaste him with all her thwarted wrath, but unfortunately for her (and most fortunate for him) the young lawyer had quickly gathered up his files from the defense table and scurried down the aisle and out into the security and anonymity of afternoon rush-hour in the city.

Having lost her whipping boy, Chris let her shoulders sag in exasperation as she swept her hand across the table, trying to locate her glasses. When was that optometrist going to have her contact lenses ready? It wasn't so much vanity as pertinacious pride that forbade her wearing her thick-framed glasses in court. But if the contacts weren't ready soon, she was going to have to break down and start wearing them even in the courtroom.

After slipping the glasses back on, she shoved her papers into her file folder and walked up the aisle of the courtroom, her thoughts distracted and rebellious. Marching through the swinging doors into the hallway, she ran into two of the men from her office.

"Hey, Chris, we didn't expect you out this soon," one of them remarked. "Don't tell us, Hamilton didn't show up again." When Chris didn't answer, he speculated further. "Surely he didn't manage to sweep you and the case under the rug in twenty minutes." As did all of the men Chris worked with, the two attorneys presented a friendly enough approach but, at the same time, maintained a tangible distance between themselves and their female colleague.

"Continuance," she sneered. "And for the record I'm not in the least worried about running up against the illustrious Warren J. Hamilton."

"Yes, but you've never yet been graced by his presence in the courtroom, either," the other lawyer commented.

"Listen," she said. "I'm convinced that he's nothing but an overblown Sergeant Buzzfuzz whose reputation is as grossly overinflated as his ego."

Chris missed the amused and perceptive look the two men gave each other, but it wouldn't have mattered anyway. She was convinced. And once Chris had come to a conclusion, she did not allow even a particle of doubt to contaminate it.

"I'll see you two on Monday." She smiled stiffly.

"Aren't you coming back to the office?"

"No, I have to run downstairs. Possession case," she grumbled.

"Narcotics?"

"Yes."

"Well, have fun," one of the men commented dryly. She smirked in reply. "Right."

Dismissing them from her mind, Chris turned away and began making her way down the long, gray, linoleum-tiled corridor, dulled and worn thin from too many years of traffic and too little wax, down the stairs into the police station, her experience in the courtroom momentarily slowing her normally self-assured stride.

Every time she thought about that obstructionist Warren J. Hamilton she became livid with anger. The man obviously thought he was Seneca, Clarence Darrow, and Perry Mason all rolled into one, and could do anything he damn well pleased.

Well, she was sick to death of this case anyway. She had been working on it for over three months now and she wanted to wrap it up. Besides, it was open-and-shut as far as she was concerned. John Anderson had been indicted by the grand jury for felonious assault and the preponderance of evidence far outweighed any possible defense that even the distinguished Mr. Hamilton could devise.

So why didn't he get on with it? Why all the postponements? Did he realize he had no chance of winning and was putting off the inevitable as long as he could? That must be it, she concluded testily. The man was, without a doubt, an egotistical coward.

By the time she reached the police sergeant's desk, she had mentally demolished any possible chance Warren J. Hamilton might have had of getting his client off. But she knew the battle was not over yet. Hamilton was still going to cause problems. That much she could morbidly sense.

The police sergeant nodded at Chris and cocked his head toward the two detectives who had their feet propped up on a long Formica-topped table. When they noticed Chris's approach, they dropped their feet to the floor and one of them stood up.

The one who was standing up had a definite leer on his face. It was an "Oh, sure, I know all about her women's-libber reputation around the station and that she's known around the D.A.'s office as a hard-nose, but I'll be damned if she isn't a fine-looking broad" expression.

She was tall and slim, but broad-shouldered, and her long stride reflected nothing short of total confidence in herself. Though her black hair was short and swept back in sleek waves, the detective imagined it would feel like silk in his hands. The strength in her body carried over to her face, manifesting itself in angular features and gleaming gray eyes surrounded by a dark fringe of lashes. There was nothing soft about this woman, but then, that was the way he'd always liked them—strong and exotic and responsive.

"Howdy, Miss Davis," the detective greeted her calmly, trying to keep a tight control over his copiously assertive male hormones.

"Detectives Billings, Stepford." She nodded at the officer who was still seated. "I understand you have a suspect for me?"

Stepford grinned lewdly and patted his knee. "Yea, sweet pea, why don't you come over here and sit on my lap and we'll discuss it awhile, okay?"

Chris scowled darkly at him, then immediately redirected her attention to the lesser of two evils—Billings. "May I see the suspect, please?" Gone was all pretense of sociability. As if weren't bad enough that the judge had called her "young lady," now this yokel had to toss on more chauvinistic drivel. *Young lady! Damn it!*

She was sick to death of putting up with all their criticisms and jokes. After all, Chris had graduated in the top third of her law-school class, and she had already begun to prove her merit as a prosecuting attorney with a successful track record of convictions.

Acutely aware of her anger, Stepford telephoned the guard to make sure the prisoner and the public defender were still waiting in Room C. The two detectives led Chris into the conference room, where she shook hands with the public defender and then sat down in a hard-backed chair across the table from a man in his early twenties, his glazed expression a mask of mute hostility.

Chris sighed with fatigue and disillusionment. "Did they read him his rights?" she asked vacantly.

14

The court-appointed attorney replied that indeed they had.

Chris studied the impassive young man across from her. "Do you understand the rights that were read to you? . . ."

Forty-five minutes later Chris walked out into the late-afternoon heat, a feeling of disenchantment coursing through every nerve in her body. The entire day had been an exercise in futility. Not only had her aggravated assault case been postponed . . . again, but she had just wasted three-quarters of an hour staring gloomily at a totally uncooperative repeat offender.

The District Attorney's office had reason to believe that he was merely a pawn in a huge narcotics smuggling operation. They felt that if they could work out a plea bargain for him and get his cooperation, the department could go after the leaders of the drug ring, who were thought to be responsible for several recent drug-related murders in the area. But so far the prisoner and his *too-inexperienced-to-know-any-better* attorney seemed totally unresponsive to such a proposition. What it boiled down to was that the kid knew in his street-wise bones that if he snitched, he was as good as dead.

The rush-hour traffic in the downtown area was beginning to swell, and Chris figured it was going to take her the better part of the hour to get home. She glanced at the slim gold watch on her wrist and sighed. Six o'clock. And Phillip was coming to pick her up at seven thirty.

Why, oh, why did she agree to go with him to this party tonight? She hated parties! It was going to be one of those insincere affairs where lawyers toasted each other's health and slapped each other's backs and then tomorrow found themselves trying to slaughter each other on the courtroom floor.

It wasn't that Chris didn't believe in being sociable. It was simply that she couldn't understand how two fiery opponents in court could walk out arm-in-arm and discuss the coming weekend's golf game, or buy each other rounds of drinks the same evening. Staying away from that type of fraternization was a matter of principle, a principle which she could not compromise.

But she had promised Phillip. He was the newest addition to the D.A.'s staff of young, bright legal minds, and he hadn't been there long enough to learn that Chris wasn't exactly the sociable type. When she turned down his invitation, he continued to pursue her until she finally agreed to go for the sole purpose of getting him off her back. She had to say one thing for Phillip—he was persistent.

By the time she had walked back to her office building, located her sports car in the high-rise parking lot, and merged into the traffic flow, it was six thirty. If she was going to eat anything tonight, she'd better stop at one of the fast-food drive-ins and grab a hamburger.

After collecting her paper bag full of cold, soggy french fries and stale hamburger, Chris pulled back into traffic, juggling the food on her lap as she drove. She gobbled it so quickly, it felt as if it were stuck in lumps in her throat and chest, and she couldn't help but wonder if all twelve billion hamburgers sold were as bad as the one she had just eaten.

Had anything gone right today?

She pulled into the underground garage of her apartment building, switched off the engine, and pulled up the parking brake of her MGA. This car was her one concession to frivolity. Black with a red interior, black canvas convertible top, Plexiglas side curtains, and silver-wire wheels, it was totally impractical, but she wouldn't and couldn't part with it. It had served her well through three years of law school and the seven months she had been practicing here with the D.A.'s office.

She walked into the elevator and pushed the button for the seventh floor. It stopped briefly in the lobby, and several tenants stepped into the elevator and greeted Chris warmly. For, to the tenants of this building, Chris Davis was only one step away from sainthood.

New owners had taken control of the property and were attempting to convert the entire building to condominiums. Thirty-five of the one hundred and ten residents were elderly couples who were barely scraping by on their Social Security checks as it was. If the building were to go condo, there would be no way most of them could afford to stay. Nor could they find another place for the same rent they had been paying.

The idea of evicting elderly people was so appalling to Chris that she had readily accepted the position of leader of the opposition. She would fight for the rights of these people, and, if necessary, she would use her own money to help pay court costs.

She had gotten nowhere talking with the executives of Co-Vestment, the corporation that had bought the building. Now she would have to go behind the scenes and talk to their lawyers.

As she slipped her key in the lock she heard her telephone ringing through the door. Quickly opening the door and rushing to the wall phone, she lifted the receiver from the hook and answered.

"Hello?"

"Miss Davis, this is Bernice in the manager's office."

"Yes, Bernice, how are you?"

"I'm fine, Miss Davis. The reason I'm calling is to tell you that a man from your office telephoned earlier with a message for you."

"Okay, what is it?"

"Wait, I'll read the message. It says 'Miss Pottsworth from Co-Vestment . . .'" Isn't that the company that's trying to take over the building?"

"Yes, Bernice, it is. What's the rest?" Chris had left a message with the secretary at Co-Vestment's main office this morning to find out the name of the firm that represented them, and knowing that she would be leaving the office early, she'd given the secretary her home phone number.

"Well . . . this Miss Pottsworth called and said, 'The firm that handles the legal affairs of Co-Vestment is Doddson and Hamilton.' That telephone number is—"

"I know the number, Bernice. Thank you." Chris slowly replaced the receiver with agonizing caution, her barely controlled temper forcibly imposing its will on the explosive reactions that were about to detonate inside her head.

Doddson and Hamilton. Warren J. Hamilton! How many times was she going to have to run up against that man? Must he have his finger in every pie in town? Oh, but she would like to meet him face to face and give him a piece of her mind once and for all.

Chris slumped into one of the rattan chairs set around her glass-topped kitchen table. The volcanic fury that swept through her body at the sound of Warren J. Hamilton's name again left her muscles weak.

She cupped her chin in her palm. Was she perhaps taking life too seriously? Was that why she always felt so tired and drained of emotion? She shook her head in bewilderment. Life was serious . . . wasn't it? After all, there was so much inequity in the world that had to be rectified. Someone had to worry about the disparity and try to resolve it. If she didn't stay involved, the Warren J. Hamiltons of the world were liable to take control. She didn't want to sit back and let that happen.

As she was forcing herself up from the chair she heard a knock at the door. Dejectedly dropping back down on the chair seat, she stared at the clock over the sink. Seven thirty. Phillip. Party. Not ready. Don't want to go. Oh, hell!

"Phillip, come on in." Chris held the door open for him and affected a genuine smile of greeting. "I just walked in the door, so I haven't had time to change."

"That's all right, we've got time."

Chris stared at him vacantly. "Well, actually, Phillip, I thought I would just go as I am. Don't you think this is okay?"

Phillip's composed expression revealed nothing as he took in Chris's severely tailored dark linen skirt and matching blazer. The only soft, feminine touch was the white silk blouse with the bow at the neck. "It's . . . you look love . . . very nice, Chris."

"Good, shall we go?" Chris was glad that little problem was settled. She wanted to get this party over with so she could get to bed at a decent hour for a change.

"I brought you a flower." Phillip pulled a small tis-

19

sue-wrapped bundle from behind his back and held it out to her.

"A flower! How thoughtful." Good grief, Chris groaned inwardly. She hadn't been given a flower by a date since she was in high school. She accepted the package and unwrapped the paper. "How nice, it's a . . . gardenia." Her smile faded. A smelly gardenia. Oh, how she hated gardenias. "Thank you, Phillip."

She was heading for the kitchen to find a glass in which to put the flower when Phillip offered, "Here, let me help you put it on."

"Oh . . . of course." She began to reel from the overpowering odor of the flower as he pinned it to the lapel of her jacket. "How lovely."

The party was to be held at the Philwood Club, an elegant bar, restaurant, and meeting place for the city's influential inner circle. When Chris and Phillip arrived, they were greeted by several colleagues from their office. Although most of the women there were dressed in slinky cocktail dresses, Chris couldn't care less. She felt more comfortable maintaining a professional appearance and she didn't particularly care if people thought her aloof or not. She certainly wasn't about to compete with other women for attention.

In contrast to the impression others had of her, Chris did not see herself as a beautiful woman. She was tall and sturdy, and she felt that her facial features reflected that durable image. But she was comfortable with her looks, and she knew she had that certain something that made her interesting and striking in her own way.

Phillip brought her a glass of white wine, and the two of them began mingling in the crowd. As she looked through the large plate glass windows overlooking downtown Tulsa, Chris was only half-aware of the tinkling of glasses and drone of chattering voices behind her.

The city strained its own back as it sprawled farther and farther in all directions. New centers for cultural or commercial or professional pursuits sprang up almost overnight, adding chrome and glass as an industrious contrast to the gracious homes and rhododendron-lined boulevards.

Chris, however, was not thinking of urban sprawl as she stared out the window, but instead of Warren J. Hamilton and how he had managed to screw up her entire day. Her hand tightened its grip on the stem of her glass as the fury spread with the wine through her bloodstream. She couldn't wait to get him into court and sink her teeth into his unscrupulous hide.

"Chris?" Phillip was waving a hand in front of her face. "Are you in there?"

She laughed without a trace of self-consciousness. "Yes, I was thinking about the Anderson case."

"I understand it was postponed again. Looks like old Warren J. is running you around the flagpole." Phillip chuckled.

"I wish I could find something humorous about it." Chris grimaced briefly before taking another sip of her wine. "If and when I ever come in contact with that man, he will learn to rue the day he ever came up against me."

"What do you mean if and when?" Phillip looked incredulous. "Isn't that the guilty party himself holding court over there in the corner?"

Chris felt a prickling sensation along her spine as if

21

every nerve ending had suddenly been activated. Wide-eyed, she turned slowly to search the corner Phillip had indicated.

Surrounded by an adoring fan club, including some of the lawyers from Chris's office, stood a man so markedly different from what Chris had expected that she could only stare.

He was tall and trim, but imposing, and imperially distinguished. Certainly not the barrel-bellied, cigar-smoking pettifogger she had pictured.

Even with her glasses on Chris squinted out of habit as she analyzed the physical attributes of her opponent.

He was much younger than she had expected. Forty at the most, she guessed. His hair was dark brown, almost black, but a few gray strands wove through the brown directly above his ears. He was tan—much too tan and healthy-looking to have spent any time in an office, incriminating evidence that he spent his days on the tennis court or golf course instead of attending to his clients and court cases. His physique attested to the fact that he was in great shape. His suit was probably custom-made, precise in cut, and the snug fit offered evidence of a broad, muscular chest.

Chris grudgingly noted a certain compelling attractiveness in the angular structure of his jaw, nose, and chin—totally relentless features. She wasn't close enough to see the color of his eyes, but she could tell even from here that they too would be just as compelling and ruthless. He was indeed going to be an imposing adversary.

But that should make no difference, she argued with herself. And, it didn't! That man had caused her more trouble than he was worth. Her free hand pressed into her waist as she debated the best course of action to take with him. She knew if she spoke to him, she would have to control her temper. She didn't want him to have any advantage over her.

With an involuntary tightening of her jaw Chris handed Phillip her glass of wine, then strode fearlessly and, she hoped, casually across the room toward the unsuspecting Warren J. Hamilton. In a totally unpremeditated and involuntary gesture (and one she would later regret), Chris removed her glasses, cautiously making her way by memory rather than by sight.

She stopped on the outskirts of his entourage, her gray eyes narrowed dangerously at Hamilton's now silent and curious expression. He had watched her approach, and his eyes expressed interest at the determined look in her eyes.

"Mr. Hamilton?" Chris smiled politely, but the smile never reached her eyes. "I'm Chris Davis. I was wondering if I might have a word with you."

She noticed that his gaze flicked over her body in quick assessment, but there was no lascivious glint in his eyes.

"My pleasure," he answered easily, and Chris realized with dismay that his quiet, deep voice had no trace of the bellowing pomposity she had expected to hear.

"In private, please," she added, as much for the benefit of the men and women standing around him as for Warren Hamilton himself.

He nodded. "Of course."

The lawyers who had been hovering around Warren like parasitic drones receded into the crowd as he and Chris strolled toward an empty space against one wall.

"Yes?" He leaned casually against the wall, but he folded his arms across his chest in an automatic gesture that Chris immediately interpreted as self-protection.

"I would like to know what you're doing with the Anderson case," she asked in a hushed voice.

"The Anderson case?" Warren's brow knitted in consternation as his mind sifted through the backlog of cases in his office, trying to place this particular one. "The Anderson case."

"Yes, Anderson. John Anderson. Aggravated assault." Chris had begun losing patience weeks ago with this legendary demigod, and finding out now that he did not fit the pigeonhole in which she had placed him did nothing to improve her temper.

"Oh, yes, Anderson. Now I recall. So, you're *that* Chris Davis." He smiled, but because she was not wearing her glasses, Chris couldn't tell if it was an ingratiating smile or not.

As he scrutinized her closely Chris felt the prickly sensation along her spine again, and she knew her words were becoming garbled and inconsistent, another thorn in her perfectionist side.

"I'm awfully tired of these postponements, Mr. Hamilton. I'm tired of getting the run-around. I'm tired of being greeted in the courtroom by your errand boys. When are you going to admit that you have no defense in this case and allow justice to be served?"

A slow, disbelieving smile crept across Warren's face. "Justice, Ms. Davis? Justice?" He shook his head with a light chuckle. "And pray tell, counselor, how do you define that term?"

"This is not a philosophical discussion," Chris shot back, unaware that her voice was carrying to a group of men standing only a few feet away. "I'm trying to tell you that I've had it with this stonewalling strategy of yours. We have a woman who claims to have been beaten by Mr. Anderson while he was attempting to rob her of her purse. We have depositions of medical experts and witnesses. And why is your firm defending this man in the first place? Mr. Anderson is an indigent, so why not let the public defender handle it?"

Not allowing him a chance to answer, Chris breathed deeply before forging ahead with her ultimatum. "Mr. Hamilton, I have requested for the last time that the judge set a trial date and I expect you to appear in court on August fifth at eleven o'clock."

At some point during Chris's tirade Warren's arms had fallen to his sides. His stance was still relaxed, but there was a wide-eyed look in his dark brown eyes that conveyed nothing short of stunned disbelief. There was also something else, a look that would have disturbed Chris even more if she had seen it. There was a kind of raw respect in his eyes that had nothing to do with his evaluation of her as a professional, but rather of her as a woman. And, there was also a deep sense of amusement.

"By all means, I will be there, Ms. Davis," Warren grinned. "Now, have you finished scolding me?"

"Yes . . . no . . . I mean . . ." Chris stammered awkwardly, then offered her first tentative smile. "That was a loaded question if I ever heard one. Is that allowed outside the courtroom, counselor?"

"Probably not," he shrugged. "But you have to admit, you deserved it."

Chris's smile began to fade. She was not going to let

25

this man get the upper hand. She had a legitimate bone of contention with him that she intended to pick clean.

"There's another point at issue between us, Mr. Hamilton." Chris began, not sure exactly which approach she should take.

"I don't suppose you're referring to the grievance of thirty-five tenants of the Willow Towers apartment complex, are you?"

Chris's gray eyes fastened on him with furious intent. This was one case about which she could not remain objective. She knew these people. They were her friends. She passed them in the hallways, helped them with their grocery bags, listened to their timeworn reminiscences over and over.

Even though Warren Hamilton's stature and experience seemed to compel a certain deference, when Chris spoke, her voice was brittle and short, like the snapping of a dry twig under too much strain.

"With regard to . . . that particular matter . . . I will not tolerate delays such as those I have been forced to endure with the Anderson case. I expect prompt action. I hope I make myself perfectly clear," she enunciated slowly, aware of a fretful beating of her heart with each syllable she uttered.

His eyes once again narrowed speculatively and he pursed his lips slightly to suppress a smile. "Perfectly," he finally answered with an amused lilt to his voice.

"Thank you for your time, Mr. Hamilton." Chris nodded in mock subservience. "Good night." Pivoting on the heels of her black pumps, she walked back across the room toward Phillip.

"Watch out for that table, Ms. Davis," he called after her just before she bumped into a low glass-topped

26

table that, in her myopic state, blended perfectly with the floor.

She stopped, her shoulders snapping to attention, and she felt the hackles rising once again at the back of her neck. Unwilling to concede the fact that Warren J. Hamilton had dealt her a crushing personal blow, Chris stoically detoured around the table, slipping her glasses on as inconspicuously as possible.

Behind her, Warren chuckled to himself. What a woman! He watched the receding straight back, the severe, almost manly linen suit, the short black hair that was sleeked back into a professional coiffure with not a single strand out of place, the determined stride and erect head. But all of this was in the periphery of his vision. His eyes were trained instead on the gentle sway of her hips beneath her skirt—an unconscious physical motion that defied all the carefully controlled restraints Chris Davis had imposed on the rest of her mind and body.

Watching her cross the room, Warren J. Hamilton smiled to himself and silently pronounced judgment in the case of *Davis versus Hamilton.*

CHAPTER 2

As the throng of disciples slowly gathered once again around their guru, Warren politely extricated himself and walked to the bar, where he picked up two glasses of wine. He then proceeded confidently toward the spot where Chris was standing by the windows.

She had been weaving her way through the crowd, looking for Phillip to take her home. The confrontation with Hamilton had given her a throbbing headache. But when she finally found Phillip, he was deeply involved in a debate with several other men over a recent Supreme Court ruling. She pulled her sleeve back to look at her watch. Had she really only been here for an hour? She knew this discussion could go on forever, especially since most of the participants in the debate were afflicted with incurable verbosity anyway.

"Looking for an escape?" Warren leaned down from behind and whispered close to her ear.

Startled, Chris twirled around to face him. She kept

28

her expression blank, but her thoughts were a whirl of suspicions as she watched him hold a glass out to her.

"Truce?" he smiled, but the curve of his mouth tightened when he received no response. "You were drinking the Chenin Blanc, I believe." He continued to offer her the glass.

At her almost imperceptible frown he shrugged. "Oh, I saw you when you first walked in and I noticed what your escort got for you at the bar. You see, I have twenty-twenty vision." Warren smiled at the pink flush that crept along the skin of Chris's neck and face. He cautiously placed the glass in her hand, making sure she had her fingers tightly gripped around it.

"I can see just fine with my glasses, Mr. Hamilton," Chris responded, still embarassed that she had let him catch her tripping over tables. She sipped reluctantly at the wine in her hands, but her eyes were cautiously watching Warren's face for hidden motives. Did he think he was going to be able to charm her into some sort of concession or plea bargain? She was sure that a man like that was used to winning by whatever means necessary. Well, she was not the kind of woman to be easily charmed by any man, even one as illustrious and urbane as Warren J. Hamilton.

"Aren't you disappointing quite a few fans over there?" Chris nodded toward the group who had been congregating around him.

"Chris—is that short for Christine?" Warren ignored her jibe and cocked his head, attempting to make polite small talk.

Chris shook her head in amused disbelief. Who did he think he was dealing with? She had heard all about his reputation as a trial lawyer. He was famous for humbling himself before a witness, pouring on the country-boy charm, then striking with the swift, deadly accuracy of a cobra whenever the witness dropped his guard.

"It's short for Chris," she answered curtly.

"Your parents named a girl like you Chris?" He seemed genuinely amazed that any marginally sane parent would do such a thing.

"Look." Chris sighed with exasperation. "I haven't been called Christine since I was five years old . . ."

"Then Chris *is* short for Christine?" He seemed satisfied with this line of questioning.

"Yes," she snapped. "It's short for Christine. Case closed."

Warren nodded and brought the wineglass to his lips. But Chris could see the smile that curved his mouth along the rim of the glass. He had won the round, and he knew it.

She was caught off guard when he suddenly wrinkled up his nose and frowned. "Did your date buy that for you?"

"What?" she asked, totally confused by his question.

"That." He pointed to the gardenia on her lapel.

Chris glanced down at the flower and wrinkled her nose as well, unable to suppress a conspiratorial smile. "I'm afraid so."

"How sweet," he muttered. "Just like the prom. Listen, why don't we tell old . . . what's your date's name?"

"Phillip?" Chris felt an automatic stiffening along her spine as she sensed that Warren had shifted the tone of the conversation to a more personal plane.

"I don't know, is it?"

"His name is Phillip, Mr. Hamilton," Chris snapped. "If there was a rising inflection in my voice, it was because I was wondering why you were asking his name, not because I didn't know his name."

"Oh," he smiled. "I see. Well, as I was saying, why don't we tell old Phillip that we have to discuss our case." He leaned closer to whisper in her ear. "That way we can get away from here."

The skin along her cheek and neck prickled where his warm breath hit it. She stepped back to ease the tension on her tightly stretched nerves. "I believe we have discussed all we have to discuss," she responded coolly, but with a slightly indulgent tone, as if she were speaking to a child. "And I certainly have no intention of escaping anywhere. I came with Phillip, and I will leave with Phillip."

"A woman of high principles," he muttered under his breath, making no attempt, however, to keep the comment from her ears.

"It appears that I'm one of a dying breed in our profession," she drawled in a voice thick with sarcasm.

Warren's jaw tightened instinctively. "Meaning?"

Immediately regretting her pompous outburst, Chris tried to come up with an answer to his question. "It just seems to me that some people will defend anyone for money."

"Is that a reference to my own practice, by any chance?"

Chris was aware of the darkening glint in Warren's eyes, and she was sorry she had ever opened her big mouth. At the same time she meant everything she had said, and there was certainly nothing wrong with standing up for one's principles.

31

"I just believe," she began tentatively, "that there are . . . certain people who should be taken out of the mainstream." Chris fought back the impulse to run. She had embarked on this line of discussion; she might as well be prepared to finish it. "And . . . certain corporations should not be allowed to exploit the needs of honest citizens . . ."

"Bravo, Christine!" Warren interrupted by setting down his glass on a nearby table and clapping his hands. "Bravo! I couldn't agree with you more. However . . . " He abruptly wiped the smile from his face and speared the air between them with his index finger. "Whether you are referring to Mr. Anderson and Co-Vestment or not, there is one thing you had better get straight from the start in this business. You are not God. Nor are you the judge or jury. So don't start moralizing about my clients. They are innocent until you prove . . . beyond a reasonable doubt . . . that they are guilty."

Chris noticed that not once had he raised his voice or changed his tone, yet she felt as properly chastised as a wayward child who had just received ten licks behind the woodshed. She was relieved to see that Phillip had finally resolved the momentous judicial question of the evening and was making his way toward her.

"Well." She tried, with little success, to sound unperturbed. "Thank you for the lecture, Professor Hamilton. Now, I guess I will see you in court on the fifth, and unless you send one of your flunkies to the Willow Towers meeting, I will see you there in two days."

Warren watched her closely for a minute before responding. "I wouldn't miss it for the world, counselor."

With that parting shot Warren turned and wended

his way back through the crowd, stopping a couple of times to chat with friends.

Chris watched him move with ease through this social world, and she envied him. Although she still hated the idea of tossing all courtroom animosities out the window the minute the trial was over, she was jealous of Warren's ability to make the transition between business and the social sphere with such ease and grace.

But envy was only a part of it. Warren J. Hamilton irritated the hell out of her. He was egotistical, overly confident, crafty, intriguing, and in all likelihood, totally unprincipled. He was also incredibly fascinating, in addition to other characteristics that, when combined, could be extremely hazardous to an idealistic, inexperienced female attorney all alone in her fight to balance the scales of justice.

Chris immediately swept away the conflict of emotions she was feeling, forcing herself to remember the trouble Hamilton had put her through and, undoubtedly, would continue to do. Don't let his inimitable style fool you, Chris. The man is a pain in the neck, period.

Damn! Damn! Damn! Chris slammed the folder shut and threw it on the far corner of her desk. She removed her glasses and closed her eyes briefly, pinching the bridge of her nose to help relieve the strain on her eyes. Why me? Why in the name of heaven did that man have to single her out for this kind of punishment?

She slipped her glasses back on and pulled the folder containing the Johnston case back from the corner, sighing with resignation over her fate. She opened it again and stared at the small slip of paper inside. The note was hastily written by Phillip and could be a mistake. Could be, but that was doubtful, she conceded. He had made a point of writing it down because he obviously thought she would find it humorous. He was wrong. She reread it for the third time. "Knew you'd be thrilled to hear that Warren Hamilton is now defending Albert Johnston. Your own personal albatross." Chris could just hear Phillip's sadistic giggle as he wrote the note.

The question was, Why Warren Hamilton? She had been working on this case for several months now, and she knew that Albert Johnston's defense was being handled by Hamilton's firm. But at the arraignment and at the hearing following the grand-jury indictment one of the associates from his firm had been there to represent their client. Why was Hamilton himself suddenly sticking his finger into this pie?

Chris lifted the receiver on her desk phone and dialed her boss's office. "Bill? This is Chris. Sorry to bother you, but do you happen to know why Warren J. Hamilton would suddenly be so interested in the case of Albert Johnston?"

"Refresh my memory, Chris." The district attorney's voice betrayed his fatigue. Everyone in this office was frazzled and Chris knew that her boss must be feeling the pressure even more. It was a basic fact of life that prosecutors lacked the time and the personnel to investigate all the crimes that came across their desks. Attempting to keep up with the case load was, at best, an exercise in futility.

"It's the embezzlement case. Johnston is a securities broker who pocketed the money of about a dozen potential investors."

34

"Oh, sure, now I recall. Well, I don't know . . . other than . . . Could be because you're on the case."

"What is that supposed to mean?" Chris asked, a chill raising tiny goose bumps along her skin.

"Oh, just a rumor I heard," he answered vaguely.

"What rumor? Come on, Bill, I really don't know what you're talking about."

"Well, someone . . . I don't remember who . . . mentioned that you and Hamilton had a run-in the other night. I heard—although I find this a little hard to believe—that you had the upper hand. Maybe Warren's just trying to even the score a bit. You're not worried about him, are you?"

"Of course not!" Chris declared, indignant that anyone would think she would back down from the likes of Warren J. Hamilton.

"Good," Bill answered seriously, but Chris was sure he was smiling on the other end of the line. "By the way, have you made your reservations for the bar association convention? It's less than a month away, remember."

"Thanks for reminding me," she responded distractedly, still thinking of Hamilton and his intrusion into this case. "I'll have to get right on that."

"Is that all you wanted to talk about?"

"Yes, Bill. Thanks." Several unladylike expletives intended to describe Warren Hamilton's character ran through Chris's mind as she replaced the receiver. The man was not only a pain in the neck, he was a pain in the . . .

Her imprecations were abruptly interrupted by two colleagues who entered her office for a meeting about an arson case they were handling. The three of them spent the next hour preparing the evidence they would be presenting before the grand jury, compiling a list of witnesses and evidence to be used in the later trial, and in general covering every angle of the case to be sure that it would not be tossed out of court on a technicality.

For Chris, this essential preparation for trial was the vital core of legal practice. The substance of law was like a living organism; the delict, or offense, was the tiny seed that ruptured into existence, legal precedents spiraled in historic procession and arranged themselves into the backbone, the construction and development of the case formed the pliable marrow, and the courtroom drama was the constitutional heart, with attorneys and judges directing each tumultuous beat.

After the two lawyers left her office, Chris's secretary came in to jot down various court dates on the desk calendar. "Don't forget the Ramirez arraignment is on the docket for tomorrow afternoon," she reminded Chris. "And the attorneys for Nastashi have filed for a continuance. Oh, and by the way Warren Hamilton called and said he'd see you at the Willow Towers meeting tonight. Chris? Chris? Are you all right?"

At the sound of that wearisome name again, Chris had dropped her head to the desk and was cradling it in the crook of her arm. After several long seconds the solicitations of her secretary finally pierced her consciousness and she lifted her head.

"I'm okay, Joan. Just tired. Very, very tired." This was a gross understatement. There was something about that man—even the mention of his name—that drained every ounce of strength from Chris's body. She had known that he would be at the meeting tonight.

But the fact that he had called to remind her made this first formal encounter between them take on a significance that she didn't want to acknowledge.

"Why don't you go home?" the secretary suggested. "It's after four. Surely you could take off a little early today."

"Yes." Chris wearily pushed herself up from her desk. "I think I will do just that. Thanks, Joan."

"Don't mention it." She handed Chris her purse and watched with a frown of concern as Chris walked out of her office looking more tired and defeated than she had ever seen her.

At seven thirty the elevator doors slid open and Chris stepped into the lobby where the tenants' meeting was to be held. Having revived herself with dinner and a shower, she was now convinced that she was ready to face anyone, including Warren Hamilton. The man was beginning to crowd her life, and she did not like that one little bit, but they *were* going to be seeing quite a lot of each other in the next few months, so she might as well get used to it.

Focusing her mind on the issue at hand, she greeted the tenants who were already there and sat down to visit with several elderly couples with whom she had become close friends.

Ten minutes passed before a vice-president of Co-Vestment and the corporation's distinguished legal counsel entered the building.

She composed her features into solid lines of disinterest when Warren walked into the room, but the warm flush that immediately suffused her skin proved traitor to her attempts at control.

He was wearing gray slacks and a summer-weight navy sport coat over a blue shirt. Under the fluorescent light of the apartment lobby his hair and eyes appeared even darker than she had remembered. Something sparked in the dark brown centers of his eyes when they first met hers, and he poked the inside of his cheek with his tongue in speculation when he noticed the fiery flush on her cheeks.

The guests were invited to help themselves to coffee and sweet rolls, which were set out on the folding table against the wall. As everyone moved in that direction Chris strode purposefully toward Warren, cutting off his route to the coffee table.

"Do you mind if I ask what you're doing?" she whispered so the others could not hear.

Genuinely taken aback by this, Warren raised his palms in supplication. "Why, I'm here to listen to the tenants' grievances against my client. I thought you wanted me to come." He put his hands on his hips and cocked his head. "Now what is our little Ms. Quixote upset about tonight?"

"I couldn't care less whether you've come or not, Mr. Hamilton. But, that's not what I'm talking about. I want to know why you are suddenly so interested in defending that embezzler Albert Johnston."

"Alleged embezzler, Ms. Davis."

"Don't lay semantics on me, counselor. I want to know why you, rather than your associate, decided to handle the case all of a sudden." Chris's jaw was tightening with every imperturbable smile that flitted across Warren's face.

"Because you are prosecuting," he said simply.

Startled by the bluntness of his reply, Chris was

struck dumb for several seconds. "What . . . what does that have to do with anything, Mr. Hamilton?"

He smiled enigmatically. "It has to do with everything, Christine."

Her name in his possession flowed as smooth as glass across his tongue, but she refused to allow that persuasive eloquence to diminish her irritation with him.

"You are becoming a nuisance, Mr. Hamilton." Chris folded her arms across her chest. "An attractive one, I'll admit. But still, a nuisance."

Warren placed a hand across his heart. "Christine, you wound me." He grinned. "But the law of trespass requires only that I exercise reasonable care in protecting someone against the dangers of attraction."

"That law pertains to property owners," she replied snidely. "And it also was enacted to protect persons who are unaware of the risks of attractive nuisances, which I most certainly am not."

Warren studied Chris for a moment, a half-smile playing around his mouth. "Listen, I've been thinking. If we're going to be running into each other all the time, maybe it would be better if we were on the same team."

Chris stared blankly for a few seconds before the enormity of what he was saying dawned on her. "Are you suggesting that I quit my job with the D.A? Work for the defense?"

He grinned. "Sure, why not?"

Her mouth was open, and she was shaking her head, but the ludicrousness of his idiotic joke had rendered her speechless. "I can think of a hundred reasons why not, but I am only going to give you one, Mr. Hamilton. I have absolutely no intention whatsoever of ever defending the likes of Co-Vestment." She cocked her head disdainfully at the corporate vice-president, who was now sidling up to some of the tenants with an obvious strain at polite conversation.

"Well, you're probably right," Warren conceded, having known ahead of time what her reaction would be to his joke. "I was only afraid that people might stop believing in the integrity of our judicial system if they got wind of our relationship and yet still saw us on opposing sides of the fence."

"Relationship!" Chris snapped. "There is no relationship, Mr. Hamilton, and there never will . . ."

"Shhh, Chris." Warren indicated the crowded room. "They might get suspicious. Listen," he said, ignoring the brittle line of Chris's mouth and the blazing fire that ignited her gray eyes. "I'll tell you what. When I'm talking tonight, don't smile too much at me or laugh too loudly at my jokes. We don't want people to suspect the truth. You know how the song goes—'People will say we're in love' . . ."

Before he could utter any more of this fatuous nonsense, Chris whirled away from him and stalked off to a chair at the back of the room, her skin tingling with the almost blind fury that boiled beneath the surface.

Of all the nerve! Of all the egotistical, presumptuous, audacious ideas! The man was obviously insane. Totally and unequivocally.

As Chris sat fuming in her chair on the back row the room suddenly came alive as if an electrifying presence had taken control. And it had, in the person of Warren J. Hamilton. Emotions were running high over this issue, yet Warren somehow managed to convey the idea that he was on everyone's side, that he understood the plight of the tenants and that he was trying to work with his client toward the most equitable solution.

Chris could feel it. She could sense the tenants softening toward Warren, and she was furious. How could they be so gullible to believe that hypocritical, double-dealing shyster!

The whole time Warren talked, Chris clenched her hands tightly in her lap, not yet daring to express an opinion, lest she do it with both her hands wrapped tightly around his throat.

He was just the type of man these older, defenseless people would adore. Dressed casually, yet neatly, in not too expensive clothes, he appeared to be the very model of the all-American male. The barely noticeable touch of gray added a calm dignity to his otherwise vigorous appearance.

It wasn't fair that a man like him, with a winning smile and a charismatic personality, could wrap his charm like a warm cloak around these people and immediately win their support on any issue. It was what had made him such a successful attorney, she knew, but it still wasn't fair. Chris worked hard—a hell of a lot harder than he did, most likely—and yet she wasn't able to twist people's thoughts around to coincide with her own. She didn't have that kind of power, and being around someone who did made her very uneasy.

In addition his sense of humor was simply too much to take. She knew that his remarks about a relationship between the two of them were nothing more than a joke, but still they had made her feel and look vulnerable and weak in front of him—the worst possible way to appear. For in law the idea was always to stay one step ahead of your adversary.

"Mr. Hamilton." Chris had risen to her feet, and Warren could doubtless feel the fire that was darting from her eyes all the way across the room. "All this talk about an equitable solution is fine, but let's be truthful, shall we? The bottom line is that we, as tenants, are going to have to pay considerably more each month for the privilege of staying here. Is that a correct assessment of the situation?"

The vice-president of Co-Vestment cleared his throat and stood up before the group. "If I might, Warren, I would like to address myself to the young lady's question . . ."

When the meeting ended, Chris reluctantly shook hands with the Co-Vestment vice-president and attempted to beat a hasty retreat to her apartment.

But when she reached the elevator, a large, tan hand grasped her elbow, spinning her around to face its owner.

"Going somewhere, counselor?" Warren smiled at Chris's discomposed expression.

"As a matter of fact, I'm going to my apartment. Good night, Mr. Hamilton."

"Don't we have some things to talk about?" he asked, refusing to loosen his grip on her elbow.

"Like what?" she sighed, trying without success to extricate herself from his grasp.

"Like us."

"Your brand of humor is wearing very thin," Chris said bleakly. "I'm tired. I've had a very busy day. I have to take depositions all day tomorrow. I have jury selection on a case Friday, so . . ."

"Have dinner with me." Without waiting for her

answer, Warren began guiding Chris toward the front door.

"I have already eaten, Mr. Hamilton!" Chris tried to resist his strength but failed again.

Warren stopped at the front door, turned her toward him, and held her other arm with the same irresistible strength. "Let's get something straight from the beginning. My name is Warren. Please use it. And *I* haven't eaten."

As she glared resentfully at him Warren opened the front door and guided Chris out onto the sidewalk and into the passenger seat of his red 1956 Thunderbird, parked brazenly along the curb.

"This is a no-parking zone," she announced authoritatively.

"Hm." He shrugged, not in the least perturbed as he peered down at the warning written in bold red letters on the curb. "So it is."

"Did you restore it yourself?" she asked admiringly, impressed by the car despite her feelings about its owner. Her wide gray eyes were examining the detailing on the dashboard, and her hand automatically ran along the leather upholstery.

"I did some myself and had the rest done in a shop," he shrugged.

"It's beautiful."

"Thank you. You like old cars?" he asked as he turned the engine over.

"I love them. And they're classics. Calling them old cars is a sacrilege. I have an MGA. Of course, that's not exactly in the same league with this one, but . . ."

"There you go," he broke in smugly.

"I beg your pardon?"

"Well, you see, we are of one mind," Warren concluded with satisfaction.

"We are certainly not." Chris countered emphatically. "We simply both like classic cars."

Warren turned his dark eyes on her and grinned. "Well, I guess that's something anyway."

Chris couldn't stop the smile that revealed beautiful, straight white teeth and a silvery sparkle in her eyes. "Yes," she conceded unexpectedly. "I suppose that's something."

"I know this probably isn't what you had in mind when I said I was taking you out to dinner." Warren was sitting across from her at a lopsided table covered with a plastic cloth. "But, I get so tired of eating typical restaurant food that I start craving home-cooked meals."

Jill's Diner served just that. Large bowls of mashed potatoes, platters of pork chops and chicken-fried steaks, side dishes of green beans and rolls.

"For example," Warren continued, "last night I had dinner with some friends and we had absolutely delicious lobster Newburg. But the whole time I was eating it all I could think about was coming to Jill's for fried chicken. You probably eat out a lot, too, don't you?" Warren asked as he buttered a roll with a huge chunk of butter. Where does he put it all? she wondered. He certainly wasn't heavy. Sturdy, yes, but there wasn't an ounce of fat anywhere as far as she could see.

"Yes," Chris drawled. "But on my salary it's not lobster Newburg. Let's see." She paused, placing an index finger against her lips. "Last night it was a cheeseburger, fries, and a small Coke."

Warren laughed easily, a rich, full-bodied sound that danced along Chris's spine. "They never have paid too well in the prosecutor's office. Maybe you really should try the defense for a while," he mused.

"Money isn't everything," she remarked sarcastically. "At least, not to me."

"Oh, that's right." He smiled cynically, taking his second pork chop off the platter. "You have ideals." His tone sharpened the last word to a knifelike edge.

"You say that as if it's a dirty word," Chris scowled. "At least I'm doing what I feel is right."

"And I'm not?" The glint of amusement faded from Warren's face.

"How can you be?" She raised her voice. "How can you represent people like that vice-president of Co-Vestment? Did you hear what he said in there tonight?" Chris placed a hand over her chest and proceeded to mock the tone and substance of the man's speech. "I, as a citizen of the greatest democracy in the world, have my inalienable rights, too. This is, after all, a capitalist society, a free society where . . ."

Warren grimaced and shook his head. "That's enough, Christine. I know he came on a little strong, but he does have a point."

"What!" Chris was outraged. "How can you sit there and tell me that his company has a right to force those people out of their homes?"

"I didn't say he had the right to force anyone out of his home, Christine. I said he has a point. It is a free society. He has the right to buy anything he wants to buy as long as the parties involved are in agreement and as long as the arrangement is reasonably equitable to all involved."

45

"Equitable, my foot," Chris snapped. "There's no such thing as equity in this country, and you know it. Not as long as companies like Co-Vestment can take advantage of helpless citizens like the Willow Tower tenants. And I certainly—"

"You're beautiful when you get on your high horse, did you know that?" Warren's face reflected the dawn of discovery, as if he were seeing her in this light for the first time.

Chris's chin snapped up in indignation and her gray eyes glazed over with ice.

"Even with your glasses on," Warren teased her while he watched at least five different emotions play across her face.

Her cheeks begin to flood with color when she realized she had left her glasses on after reading the menu. How could she let something like that bother her? Why did she care if he saw her with her glasses? And why was he saying things like that to her? Beautiful? She wasn't beautiful, and he knew it. "I am not beautiful, Mr. Hamilton."

"Warren. And you are beautiful. Besides that, you're extremely intelligent. A trifle stubborn, perhaps, but still . . ." He let his words trail off as his masterful gaze swept over her face. She sat there helplessly as he devoured every feature, feeling herself turned inside out for his inspection.

She rarely let men come even this close to her. She didn't want one of them invading and dismantling the pristine, ivy-mantled tower that surrounded her. Within the walls she had erected, she could slay all the dragons she wanted and still maintain her aloof detachment.

Everything she had accomplished, she had done alone, without help, without shaking the foundations of her ideals. She was achieving what she had set out to do, and she did not need or want a man like Warren Hamilton to enter her carefully structured life.

"I think . . . I'd like to go home now, Warren." Chris's voice was softer than normal, and she felt unsure of herself for the first time in her adult life.

Warren watched her carefully, taking note of the deeply troubled emotions that were visible beneath the surface of her carefully composed face. She was different from most women. He knew that. And he would have to tread very carefully into her life. His forte was the power of persuasion, and he had just received his greatest challenge.

"All right, Christine. But let me give you a small piece of advice."

"The name is Chris."

"As I was saying, Christine." He dragged out the name. "Don't get so caught up in your crusade for truth, justice, and the American Way that you make the same mistake as Don Quixote."

Her head was tilted back at an arrogant angle as she waited for his explanation.

"Don't see villains where there are really only windmills."

Chris inhaled deeply as Warren's soft-spoken advice penetrated her mind, and when she let the breath out, it had a loose, shredded sound, as if it had been ripped from the seams deep within her, unraveling the mantle of perfection she always wore. Staring across the table at that attractive, powerful face, Chris felt the first cold chunk of stone chip away from her insular tower.

CHAPTER 3

Chris sat back down at the prosecution table and donned her tortoiseshell glasses. "Well," she sighed. "I can't wait to see this."

The young associate who sat next to her leaned closer. "What's that?"

"I'm just wondering what our infamous colleague from the distinguished firm of Shyster, Badger, and Loophole will do to the jurors we want."

The other attorney shook his head and chuckled. "Well I can tell you for sure, Hamilton's not going to let us have that little gray-haired Sunday-school teacher."

He didn't. As Warren stood to survey the group of potential jurors for the John Anderson aggravated assault case, his first thought was that the sweet little old gray-haired lady must go. She would be his first peremptory challenge of the morning.

Warren glanced at Chris with an arrogant smirk, and

without a doubt she knew exactly what he was thinking. The Sunday-school teacher was a goner.

"Would you look at what that man is wearing," Chris said, holding her mouth in a tight line of disgust. "He looks as if he ordered that suit straight from a mail-order catalogue."

Her associate grinned. "That's his style, didn't you know?"

"Style? You call that rumpled-suit-look 'style'?" she smirked.

"Part of the secret of Hamilton's success is his ability to become one with the jurors."

"The common-man touch, you mean?"

"Exactly," the young man whispered. "How many of those jurors do you think have the money to pay for Pierre Cardin suits?"

"But surely those people can't be fooled by that folksy stuff!" she whispered back, outraged that Warren could get away with such tactics, and a little angry that she hadn't thought of them herself. "Any minute now I expect him to sit back down and prop his feet up on a pickle barrel while he chats with them."

"You see," the associate laughed. "Now you're thinking along Hamilton's lines."

"The only other thing missing that I can see," Chris added disdainfully, "is the straw sticking out from between his teeth."

As the morning progressed, Warren systematically eliminated any potential jurors who might be harboring any bias against his client or who should not be included for the simple reason that Chris wanted them. If she wanted them on the jury, they most likely would pose problems for him.

When she wasn't watching Warren, which was rare, and feeling the presence of him with every nerve in her body, Chris was exchanging wry glances with her associate over the diminishing number of favorable jurors.

At the conclusion of the voir dire Chris scratched through six names on the list, three had been eliminated on peremptory challenges, and she had asked the judge to eliminate three for cause of possible bias. As she handed the new list to her associate, she shrugged, knowing that as fundamental as jury selection was to the trial, she would have to accept a certain amount of compromise.

The unsuitable prospects then followed the bailiff offstage to await their fates. Some would undoubtedly return to their homes, greatly relieved that they were free from service. Others would be forced to endure more interrogations by demanding attorneys in another jury selection process.

After the panel of twelve jurors who would sit in judgment in this case had filled the box, Chris removed her glasses and stood to address them.

She knew that Warren was probably going to put on a theatrical performance for the jury. But she was not. It simply wasn't her style. Besides, there wasn't much point in wasting her best lines on her opening statement to the jury. She would save the dramatic flair for the trial itself.

As she took the first step toward the expectant jurors, she felt a hand clasp tightly on her elbow, steering her slightly toward the left. She swiveled her head, finding herself nose to chest with Warren Hamilton. He smiled benevolently and whispered, "The jury is over to your left at ten o'clock."

"I do not need a seeing-eye dog, Mr. Hamilton," Chris hissed.

"I just didn't want to see you embarrass yourself in front of the jury by tripping over a table," he whispered defensively.

"Of course not."

His eyes widened innocently as he backed away, hands up in capitulation, leaving her to her own devices.

Of all the nerve, she thought with distaste. Well, she would show him. No way was that man going to get the upper hand in this courtroom.

She strode briskly to a spot four feet in front of the jury, and, straightening her shoulders and clearing her throat ceremoniously, she began her opening remarks.

"The case we will bring before you is a fairly simple one. A man is accused of assaulting a woman while he was robbing her of her purse. The state believes and will attempt to prove that the accused held a knife at the victim's back, grabbed her purse, then pushed her forcefully to the ground, thus causing her to break her hip. The state will attempt to prove that the defendant did, with full knowledge and willful intent, commit the crime of aggravated assault. As opposing counsel will no doubt . . . dramatically inform you, the state must prove these facts to you beyond a reasonable doubt." Chris turned to smile sweetly at Warren, and to her consternation he smiled back. Stiffening her spine, she turned back to face the jurors. "That, ladies and gentlemen, we are prepared to do. And, if we do so, and if there is no reasonable doubt in your mind that the defendant committed this crime, you must, by your sworn duty, return a verdict of guilty."

Warren watched the straight, declarative line of Chris's body as she pivoted and paced, orated to the jurors with her arms and the tilt of her head. He noticed the severe cut of her suit, and he knew it was not going to be easy to cut through that icy facade and to find the warm, womanly core beneath. It was there, that much he knew. And it was going to be a provocative challenge finding it.

While she talked, Chris felt the heat from Warren's stare. Every gesture she felt was being analyzed, every word dissected. What did he think of her? And why should she care? Why, whenever he was around her, did she feel as if she were being probed and dissected like some persecuted amphibian in a biology lab?

She didn't particularly like him, she was sure of that. And he couldn't possibly care for her either. Aside from their love of antique cars and their choice of the same career, they had absolutely nothing in common. The man was completely arrogant, self-centered, unprincipled, and, with his "good old boy" routine, he behaved more like a frustrated actor than a respectable member of the legal profession.

After completing her opening remarks to the jury, Chris watched with disgust as Warren stood up and, once again, took command of the entire room. He was in his element, Chris noted, expounding the virtues of the criminal justice system, in which "every person brought before this court is entitled to .... no, demands ... a fair trial. Where a man is innocent until proven guilty. *Proven,* my friends, that is the key word. The prosecutor must prove"—Here, his voice dropped lower—"beyond a reasonable doubt that the defendant is guilty if you are to return such a verdict. However

. . ." Warren stared so intently at the jurors that each one of them must surely have felt that they had been chosen by God to bear witness to a new commandment. "If there is a reasonable doubt in your minds that my client could have committed such a heinous crime. . . .

At this point Chris had to forcefully restrain herself from rolling her eyes. The man was being tried for aggravated assault, for goodness' sake, not some satanic mass murder. But Warren was a consummate actor. This much she already knew, and inflated superlatives and explosive adjectives were the tools of his trade.

"If you hold this doubt in your hearts, ladies and gentlemen," he continued, pointing an incriminating finger at the jurors, "then you must do your sworn duty to God and this country and find the defendant innocent of the charges."

Finishing his well-practiced spiel to the jurors, Warren turned to Chris, cocking his head only slightly and smiling with such arrogance and certainty that Chris felt the blood pounding indignantly against the surface of her skin, radiating outward until she was suffused with its heat.

Relieved that a recess had been called until two o'clock, Chris donned her glasses and made her way out into the corridor, stopping at the water fountain to moisten her dry throat. Straightening and turning too quickly, she rammed into the hard frame of Warren's body. Two strong arms automatically reached out to catch her, their touch activating a flow of electricity so powerful that the muscles of her legs seemed to disintegrate and she almost slipped to the floor.

"Christine! Are you all right?" Warren's voice tightened with concern.

Shaking off the unsettling sensation of having been touched by something other than a mere mortal, Chris quickly regained the use of her muscles and employed them to break free from the suffocating grasp of Warren's arms.

"I'm fine!" She burst out of his grasp with such force that she stumbled backward a few steps. "If you hadn't been standing so close, I wouldn't have lost my balance in the first place. Do you always—"

"Christine, don't." Warren closed the space between them, the palm of his hand cupping her cheek and chin. "Don't lash out at a windmill, my little quixotic idealist." The pressure of his fingers on her face increased, and she sensed a growing tension in his body. "Do not continue this attempt to slay my image in your mind. Despite what you would like to believe, I am not the embodiment of all evil, and I won't tolerate this noble aloofness of yours for long."

"Don't try to dictate the way I should see you, Warren. I'm a grown woman, capable of making my own decisions."

"And how do you see me?" Warren folded his arms across his chest, a complacent smile curling his lips.

Unable to let such an opportunity pass, Chris breathed deeply and smiled sadistically. "If you really want to know, counselor, I find you egotistical, hypocritical, unscrupulous, and . . . and . . ."

"Come on, Christine," Warren chuckled. "Surely you can think of more than that. Shall I give you a few hints? How about malignant, hideous . . ."

"Insane," Chris added, laughing lightly over Warren's assessment of his own character.

"Oh, yes," Warren nodded his head in agreement. "That's a good one. Non compos mentis."

"And a nuisance." Chris shifted her gaze to the floor, suddenly uncomfortable with the meaningful silence that filled the space between them. Why did she lose every argument she started with this man? And why, for God's sake, did she always have this unsettled, displaced feeling when she was around him?

"I will not contest that accusation, Chris." Warren moved relentlessly closer to his target, inescapably closing more than just the physical space between them. "And I will continue to be a nuisance." Again he clasped her chin between his strong fingers. "I am hereby serving notice, counselor, that I will continue to pursue you at a more aggressive pace in the future."

She could feel the erratic pounding of her heart against her rib cage, and she was aware of a light film of perspiration at the back of her neck. She had never felt such a strange mixture of anticipation and alarm in her life. "For how . . . long?" Her breath stuck in her throat.

"For as long as it takes, Christine. For as long as it takes." His dark eyes were boring into her, and she felt as if he had begun to systematically tear away at the foundation of her impregnable fortress. It was, without question, the strangest, most exhilarating moment of her life.

"Excuse me, Mr. Hamilton." A young man in a natty three-piece suit cleared his throat, nervously trying to capture Warren's attention.

Warren's gaze shifted with a glare to the young man,

and he removed his fingers from Chris's chin. "What is it, Brian?" he asked in a gruff voice.

Brian fumbled with the file in his hand, flipping agitatedly through the papers, and in the process dropping several to the floor. "Damn," he mumbled. "Oh, excuse me, ma'am."

Chris stooped to pick them up, but Brian dropped down to intercept her.

"Don't bother with those, ma'am," he stuttered, grappling awkwardly with the loose sheets of papers.

Chris could hear Warren chuckling overhead. "You're a big help," she chaffed in rebuttal to his laughter.

"Brian, if you'll get off the floor, I'll introduce you." Warren was still laughing deep in his throat as the flustered clerk stood up with his arms full of crumpled papers. "Christine, this is Brian Fuller, a new clerk with our office. Brian, this is Ms. Davis, a colleague."

"Hello, Brian." Chris smiled politely, feeling a bit sorry for the disheveled and flustered young man.

"Oh, hello, Miss Davis. I didn't realize this was a business conversation . . . I'm sorry I had to . . ."

"What is it you wanted, Brian?" Warren asked, drumming his fingers impatiently on the wall beside the water fountain.

"Oh, well, it's these damn depositions that we took yesterday afternoon. Excuse me, Miss Davis."

Warren sighed. "Go on, Brian."

"Well, several of the transcripts include the same damn name. Excuse me, ma'am. And, well, hell, I thought maybe we should subpoena this guy, but Jones and Crawford think that's a bunch of crap . . . oh, excuse me, ma'am. But, Mr. Hamilton, I told them that

I definitely thought we should damn well subpoena the bastard . . . oh, excuse me, Miss Davis . . ."

Chris had been watching it coming. Warren's face was growing tighter with each passing second that Brian talked, and now he had finally had enough. His jaw had tightened ominously, and dark thunderclouds appeared to be gathering in his eyes. "Fuller, if I hear you say excuse me one more time to Ms. Davis, I will personally cram my cursed fist down your cursed throat. You do not need to apologize to Ms. Davis, as I'm sure she has heard of subpoenas and depositions . . . and bastards before."

Chris couldn't suppress the laugh that bubbled up from her chest. Poor Brian just stood there looking so pathetically humiliated.

She glanced at Warren, feeling a rather disturbing sense of respect for him over the way he handled the situation. He was the first man she had ever known who treated her quite naturally as an equal. And yet the most disquieting realization was that she was not his equal. No matter how he treated her in public, she knew, beyond a shadow of a doubt, that as far as the game of law was concerned he was the master and she merely a novice.

Warren was watching her closely, and she felt that he sensed this softening in her attitude toward him.

"I'm sorry, sir." Brian was practically groveling at the man's feet. "Anyway, it'll be a cinch to find the guy. He works at . . ."

"Brian." Warren's voice sliced the air with quick incisiveness. "I neglected to mention a few moments ago that Ms. Davis is with the D.A.'s office."

"Oh. Oh!" Brian's eyes widened as he realized the

information he was about to give would surely aid and abet the prosecutor's case.

Chris smiled sweetly. "It's quite all right, Brian. Don't mind me. Just go ahead and . . ."

"Like hell he will," Warren boomed. "And don't expect me to apologize, Ms. Davis." Turning to Brian, he dismissed him with a wave of his hand. "We'll talk later, Brian. Right now Ms. Davis and I are going to have lunch—"

Chris interrupted hotly. "I beg your . . ."

"—at the Windsor Club," Warren finished, not even looking in Chris's direction, but instead watching Brian hurry down the hall, wrestling all the way with the file in his hands.

Her mouth snapped shut, her indignant refusal to join him smothered within her throat. The Windsor Club! She had never dreamed in a million years she would be invited there. It was known as the haven for the elitest of the elite, gathering place of prestigious attorneys, and judges, and Tulsa oil men, a male bastion against the winds of change and progress. She should decline. She really shouldn't go. How could she even consider the possibility of entering such a chauvinistic den of inequality? What was happening to her morals, to her individualism? But to have the opportunity to be one of the first women to go there . . .

"I didn't think they allowed women in there," she remarked in a weak voice, knowing that the decision to go or not to go was already out of her hands.

"Well, they will now, won't they?" Warren tilted his head to one side as he noticed the strange play of emotions crossing her face. "Surely you're not afraid of a few harmless old men are you, Christine?"

"Certainly not!" she huffed, straightening her spine and chin. "I wouldn't be standing here talking to you if that were the case, now would I?"

Warren nodded. "Touché. But I hardly think that I qualify for grandfatherly status. I assure you the gray in my hair is due solely to long years without the soft touch of a woman to ease the signs of age."

"You seem to have survived it all right," Chris pointed out. "And I hardly think that you've lived all forty years as a celibate." She knew for a fact that that wasn't true. She had heard about the throngs of women who flocked around him, responding to that indefinable aura he had.

"How did you know I was forty?" He leaned against the wall with one arm, hovering over Chris and pressing her farther under his dominion.

"I . . . I did some checking around," she muttered, silently cursing herself for falling into that trap.

"I'm flattered that you were so interested, Christine," he said softly.

"Don't be. It was simple . . . curiosity and nothing more."

He smiled. "Well, that too is something."

"What do you mean that too?"

"We both have a passion for old . . . sorry, classic cars and . . . you are curious."

"What are you doing, keeping a running tally of everything I say to you?"

"Yes," he said simply. "Everything you say and everything you do. I warned you, Christine. You are dealing with a very persistent man. When I see something I want, I go after it."

"What . . . what could I possibly have that you

. . ." As she watched one side of Warren's mouth slant upward in a tantalizing smile, Chris was aware of a flash of heat licking like flames through her bloodstream, melting every atom of resolve and honorable intention in her mind.

Fifteen minutes later, Chris entered the dark, dignified foyer of the Windsor Club, where heavy plates of armor hung like sentries on the fabric-covered walls, and carved wooden chairs lined the hallway like an empty jury box, waiting to be filled with accusing faces that would pass judgment on all who entered. She could hear the low rumble of male voices exchanging their cultivated views on the state of man, she could smell the authoritative scent of heavy tobacco in the air, and she felt more out of place than she ever had in her entire life.

As she walked by Warren's side into the inner temple of the lounge all conversation ceased. It was as if her entrance had tripped a switch that automatically cut off the sound. Only the dull roar of disbelief reached her ears.

Chris tensed and glanced sideways at Warren, ready to suggest that they turn right around and, with as much dispatch as possible, flee the premises. His expression was glowing with undisguised amusement, but when he noticed her taut features, he firmly grasped her elbow and propelled her into the room at his side. "Loosen up, darlin'," he whispered in her ear, "or they might get the idea that you're afraid of them."

That remark was all it took to change Chris's mind. With fresh courage and determination, she stiffened her back and lifted her head up in haughty surveyal of the room and its stunned occupants.

"Warren!" The booming voice of an elderly gray-haired man commanded the attention of Chris's companion. The venerable old man was perched, like Solomon before his court, in an overstuffed leather chair in front of the empty fireplace. "Well," the voice rumbled from somewhere deep inside of him. "This is quite a . . . surprise, isn't it? Who may I ask is your young lady friend?"

Warren winked at Chris to help relieve some of the tension. "Joseph," he began, as if speaking to some great patriarch. "This is Christine Davis, a prosecutor in the District Attorney's office. Christine, this is Joseph Rodale, attorney and senior partner of Payton and Rodale."

"Ex-attorney, Warren. I retired fifteen years ago, you know." The crotchety old man turned his attention to Chris, narrowing his age-rimmed eyes as he critically observed the arrogant tilt of her head. "Prosecutor, hm?"

"That's correct," she answered, biting her tongue to hold back the almost automatic "sir."

"Hm," he repeated. "In my day women were bred to gentler occupations than dealing with the coarse, brutal side of life." He began chewing on the inside of his cheek as he mused. "Nature hasn't exactly tempered the fairer sex to courtroom conflicts any more than it has for physical combat. Am I right, Warren?"

Warren smiled to himself as he took note of the rigid line of Chris's mouth and the tight set of her jaw. "Oh, I don't know, Joseph. I've known several women I would be wary of opposing either in court or on a battlefield."

"Hm," the old man grumbled. "Young lady, are you pestering Warren in order to assure a place for yourself in his law firm?"

Chris's mouth dropped open in stunned disbelief and a thunderous cloud of anger billowed upward, darkening her eyes.

If Warren had not tactfully steered her over to the bar at that very moment, Chris most likely would have been obliged to plead justifiable homicide.

"Would you care for a drink?" Warren asked in a soft, gentle voice, dipping his head down toward hers.

"Yes," she snapped impatiently. "A double."

"Double what?" he chuckled.

"Double anything, and stop laughing at me unless you're willing to handle my defense when I'm indicted for murdering that crusty old curmudgeon."

Warren was no longer trying to stifle his laughter, and the rich sound of it vibrated along Chris's nerve ends as he handed her a double scotch on the rocks.

She stared dumbly at the amber liquid in the glass. "I hate scotch."

She looked up at Warren to see if he had heard her and saw that he was laughing—at her. "Why did you get this for me?" Her gray eyes narrowed intently.

He looked around the dimly lit, smoke-filled room, then back at Chris, and raised his glass to toast her.

"Welcome to the world of men." He took a sip from his glass as he watched her closely over the rim.

"Is that what you think?" she asked. "That I want to be thought of as one of the boys?"

"I don't think that at all, Christine. I think . . . I'm

sure that you want to be seen as a beautiful, intelligent woman. However . . ." He raised a hand to stop whatever she was about to say. "I do think that somewhere along the road to success, your wires have been crossed."

"What in God's name is that supposed to mean?" she asked impatiently, tasting the scotch and making a horrible face, then setting the almost full glass on the bar.

"It means that at the rate you're going, you're destined to end up like that bullheaded octogenarian over there." Chris followed Warren's eyes toward the old man who had so grandly infuriated her a few moments ago.

She looked back at Warren, a troubled frown creasing her brow. "That's typical, isn't it?" she lamented. "If a woman tries to be assertive and get ahead in the professional world, she's thought of as masculine, or bitchy, or nasty and aggressive."

"I suppose some men look at it that way," he conceded. "I don't. But I also know that to be a good lawyer you don't have to deny the fact that you're a woman." He watched the swift denial flash into her eyes, but he snuffed it out before she had a chance to speak. "Come on, let's go outside." Warren took her arm and led her through the french doors to the deck beyond.

It was pleasant out, cooler than the average August midday in Oklahoma, and Chris was relieved to be out here alone, away from the overstuffed, pedantic atmosphere of the lounge.

The deck overlooked a small pond surrounded by a sloping hill of bermuda grass and one of the luxury housing developments that abound in the city.

It was often said that Tulsa was the wealthiest city per capita in the United States. Ranking among the world's foremost gas and oil centers, it seemed to have been spawned from black gold, generating a housing industry that specialized in several acre estates and attracted citizens whose tastes leaned toward the good life.

The city was built by men—oil men, ranchers, engineers—and it had stubbornly held on to the old ways.

"One thing you've got to learn, Christine," Warren continued, without loosening his hold on her arm. "Is that communication is a two-way process. Those men in there feel awkward in the presence of a professional woman. They don't know how they're supposed to act. You've got to show them."

"How am I supposed to show them when they don't take me as seriously as they do you or any other male attorney who comes in here?"

"Christine . . ."

"Do you know that I have had judges tell me to smile in court because women are supposed to smile. Or lawyers I work with tell me we should talk over a particular case between the sheets. Or . . ."

Chris's words were smothered inside her mouth as Warren's arms slowly encircled her and his lips gently but firmly closed over hers. It was the simple union of his mouth against hers, and yet every cell in her body reacted to the taste and scent and feel of him, to the beat of his heart so near her own.

She felt a disquietening letdown when the pressure of his mouth lessened and he stepped backward.

There was a long moment of awkward silence while

they listened to the shallow rhythm of their breathing as it slowly eased into normalcy.

"Why did you . . . do that?" Chris's voice was almost lost in her breathlessness.

"It was the only way I could think of to calm you down."

"It didn't work," she murmured self-consciously.

They both shifted uneasily.

"I feel like I'm seventeen years old again." Warren's gaze moved restlessly across Chris's face, then off into the woods beyond the deck.

"You don't look seventeen."

"Thank God." He laughed, easing the tension between them. "You should have seen me then. Tall and skinny and constantly tripping over my two left feet."

"Sounds like the entire male contingent of my senior class," Chris remembered. She sighed heavily, looking back through the doors of the lounge. "Well, I guess we'll give them something to talk about for a while, won't we?"

"Christine, I know you probably think I'm no different from any of them." Warren cocked his head toward the lounge. "But I'm not. I know it's tough for you, and I really want to help."

Her voice tightened with scorn. "You mean if people think we're having an affair, then I might be accepted in this profession?"

"That's not what I meant and you know it," he snapped back. "I want to be your friend."

"Oh? And you always kiss your friends the way you just kissed me?"

"That kiss had nothing to do with our friendship."

65

"And just what did it have to do with?" Her voice rose boldly.

Warren's masterful gaze captured her face, her attention, and her will. "I think you know the answer to that question yourself." The echo of his richly vibrating words plunged into the deepest part of her, stirring the most elemental embers of her physical being into a flickering flame of desire.

CHAPTER 4

"Objection!" Chris was on her feet in an instant. "Counsel is clearly leading the witness."

"Sustained."

Warren half-turned toward Chris and nodded, a slight quirk to his lips showing that he found her objection amusing. "I'll rephrase the question, Your Honor."

Chris sat down, pleased that for once in this trial she had not been overruled. She wasn't about to let Warren get away with anything. As was always the case with counsel for the defense, he had every advantage that the system could offer. And her job was to make sure he did not run away with it.

Warren continued to cross-examine the state's star witness in the case against John Anderson. The fifty-five-year-old woman on the stand was the victim of an assault that had broken her hip and forced her to forfeit her welfare check to her assailant.

"Now, Mrs. Romanowski," Warren said softly and gently to the witness. "Let's try this again. You say you were lying on the sidewalk, on your left side, facing the street. Is that correct?"

The woman nodded.

"I didn't hear your answer, Mrs. Romanowski."

"Yes, yes, my side." She spoke brusquely and impatiently, growing wearier by the minute with the dragging wheels of justice.

"Your left side, facing the street?"

"Yes."

"Mrs. Romanowski, you have stated before this court that the assailant pressed the tip of a knife into your back with his right hand, grabbing your purse with his left."

Chris tried to keep her mind on the proceedings, but with Warren standing before her, she was finding it increasingly difficult. Dressed again in his mail-order suit, he looked not only folksy but charming as well.

Chris glanced at the jurors to try and gauge their reaction to him and to the defendant. They didn't represent Middle America as much as she would have liked. During jury selection she had tried to retain as many of the blue-collar veniremen as she could. She wanted those who adhered to the law as closely as their circumstances permitted, who knew the meaning of hard work, and who worried about the criminal element in their own neighborhoods. Warren, on the other hand, had chosen mostly college graduates, liberals, and women. Eight women and four men. How had she let Warren finagle that? She could see the flickering interest in their eyes every time he walked by the jury box. And the defendant too was a man; not as attractive as Warren, but still, he was poor and defenseless against a system that had been prejudiced against him since the day he was born. It was not going to be easy to win this case. In fact, it was going to be tough as hell.

Warren's voice droned on with the facts of the case. "You then fell on your left hip while the assailant fled the scene behind you. Am I stating the facts correctly so far, Mrs. Romanowski?"

She nodded, then remembered this brash young man's insistence that she say it aloud. "Yes."

Chris could sense Warren moving in for the kill, and she began to perspire. If he crushed her star witness's testimony, she would have no case. "Mrs. Romanowski, how—since as you've said the man with the knife was behind you at all times—how could you see the assailant's face?"

Mrs. Romanowski shifted uneasily in the witness stand. She pointed a shaking finger at the defendant. "That's the man . . . he come at me with knife . . . he take my money . . ."

A current of agitated voices rumbled through the courtroom gallery. When order was restored, Warren continued.

"I asked you how you could identify a man who was behind you the whole time. How you could see the face of an assailant who fled the scene before you could turn around?" Warren's voice had risen several decibels, and the woman on the stand was staring in shock at the man who had spoken so nicely to her a moment ago. "Do you have eyes in the back of your head?"

"Objection, Your Honor," Chris protested.

"Overruled."

Warren continued without missing a beat. "Isn't it

true in fact that you never once saw your assailant's face? Didn't you want to punish someone so badly that you picked an innocent man out of the crowd of bystanders and—"

"Objection!" Chris was again on her feet, slamming her hand against the Formica-topped table in front of her. "Counsel is badgering the witness as well as making preposterous conjectures that clearly have no basis in testimony."

"Sustained." The judge peered over the rim of his glasses at Warren. "Counsel will refrain from indulging in such conjecture."

Warren's aggressive gaze passed from the judge to the witness to Chris. He shook his head in disgust and returned to his table. "No further questions, Your Honor."

Chris was walking down the long hallway with a couple of young attorneys from her office. They had grabbed a quick bite to eat at the cafeteria up the street and now were heading back to the courtroom for the afternoon session.

Chris had been quieter than normal through lunch, and her co-workers knew why. "Look, Chris, you did all you could. You presented all the evidence we had. The state just had to rest its case."

Her response to her colleagues' support was a sullen scowl.

"It'll pick up this afternoon," one of the attorneys insisted, despite his own uneasy feelings about the trial.

Chris looked down at the floor and shook her head lethargically. "He's going to walk. I know it. Anderson's going to walk."

At the gentle nudge of her associate Chris glanced up to see Warren Hamilton walking down the hall in their direction. He was deep in conversation with another lawyer so he didn't notice Chris until he was a few feet in front of her. When he saw her, he stopped talking and quickly and convincingly extinguished the spark that ignited in his brown eyes the moment they sighted her. Composing his features into a mask of refined courtesy, he smiled ambiguously. "Good afternoon, counselor. Ready to enter the merciless forum of justice?"

Chris's eyes locked with Warren's, and she was aware of the seductive pulse that moved in undulating waves between them. Yet she too had rearranged her expression into one of reluctant civility in an attempt to ground the electrical charge that had flared up between them. "Justice, counselor?" She raised her eyebrows in dubious speculation. "I would say that remains to be seen."

A frown flitted briefly across his brow, but it was quickly concealed behind the mask of self-control. Nodding politely, Warren crossed the hall and opened the door to the courtroom. He glanced back at Chris, but neither of their expressions revealed any emotion at all. He turned around and walked through the door, letting it swing closed behind him.

Chris expelled a long, slow breath. She had to stop thinking of Warren as anything but an opponent in this case. If only she could forget the taste and feel of his lips that afternoon at the Windsor Club. Though two days had passed, her mind and body still retained the indelible imprint of his touch. And now this! Now she would have to confront him every day in the courtroom, engage him in nothing more or less than an adversary relationship. Even more at stake was her own need to remain emotionally independent, free from any kind of personal entanglement. Ladies had no business in the courtroom, or so a judge had once told her. Well, she was a lawyer—first and foremost. Whatever else she was would have to remain hidden from Warren and from herself.

"You say that policemen sometimes lie. Have you ever been lied to by a policeman?" Chris was smiling sweetly as she cross-examined this bleeding heart that the defense was calling an eyewitness.

"No." The young man being question responded with cocky insolence.

"Then what makes you say that policemen lie?"

"Because I read about things like that in the newspaper."

"Oh," she said mockingly. "I see." Chris moved over to face the jurors, looking at each of them as she spoke to the witness.

"The police officer . . . Officer Brown, whose service record is impeccable and whom you heard earlier in this courtroom, testified that he saw the defendant attempting to run from the scene of the crime, and that he found a knife on the person of the defendant."

At this point Chris turned back to the witness. "Now, are you telling the court that Officer Brown . . . who has been on the force for thirteen years and has been decorated for heroism four times . . . is lying?"

"I'm not sure," the young man stammered.

Chris sighed dramatically. "You're not sure?"

"I mean that I think he was looking for an easy collar and—"

"Oh, now you're an expert on the psychology of a police officer!"

"No, I just—"

"Isn't it true, Mr. Tomball, that two months ago you were detained in a department store by a police officer who suspected that you had been shoplifting?"

"Objection!" Warren protested loudly.

"Overruled," the judge responded.

"And isn't it true, Mr. Tomball, that you now have it in for all policemen, that you are willing to find any excuse to discredit one, even willing to go so far as to refute the testimony of an outstanding police officer who had arrested the perpetrator of a crime of which you were a witness?"

"No!" the young man cried indignantly. "I merely wanted to—"

"No further questions, Your Honor," Chris interrupted hotly. As she sat down at the prosecution table she turned to Warren with a triumphant nod. He merely stared back, then shook his head with disdain.

As the day dragged on Chris found it more and more difficult to remain in Warren's presence. Not only did she have to watch him destroying her entire case, she had to feel herself responding to every intonation of his voice and his eyes and hands stroking her from all the way across the room.

His defense was based upon two solid premises. One, that the victim could not possibly have seen the assailant, who was behind her at all times. Two, that an eyewitness whose testimony could not be discredited saw the assailant run away from the scene of the crime *before* the police arrived. Throughout the trial he had insisted that the distraught victim had automatically pointed the finger at the defendant, who happened to be carrying a knife—a defendant who was poor, frightened, and himself a victim of a prejudicial system.

"Does the prosecution wish to cross-examine the defendant?" the judge asked as the trial was nearing an end.

"Yes, Your Honor, it does." Chris removed her glasses and rose from behind the prosecution table. At first she had wondered why on earth Warren wanted Anderson to take the stand, but now she knew why. On direct examination he had proven to be a soft-spoken, longtime victim of the American economic system, just the kind of defendant this particular jury would feel sorry for.

Chris took a deep breath and walked toward the witness stand. It was her last chance; she had to find the flaw.

"Mr. Anderson, you have been unemployed for eight months, is that correct?"

"Well, I dunno. I s'pose it's been that long."

Chris walked back to the table and glanced down at her notes, reading aloud, " 'I quit my job just before Christmas.' Those were your words, Mr. Anderson. That is eight months. Eight . . . long months without a salary. Are you receiving unemployment benefits?" she asked, knowing in advance that he was not.

"No."

"Why?"

"I dunno."

"You don't know," Chris sarcastically repeated.

74

"Didn't you ask? Didn't you go to the State Employ-ment Commission and apply for unemployment?"

"Yea."

"And what did they say, Mr. Anderson?"

"They said I wasn't eligible."

"I see." She smiled inwardly, knowing that if Warren didn't object, she would have the defendant spilling his guts. "Then will you please tell the court and the jury why you are not eligible for unemployment?"

"Objection!" Warren jumped from his chair and glared at Chris. "Your Honor, the prosecution is pur-suing a line of questioning that is clearly irrelevant and prejudicial to my client."

"Approach the bench," the judge ordered wearily, removing his glasses and wiping the lenses with the sleeve of his robe.

As Chris stood before the judge's bench her hand accidentally brushed against Warren's, and she jerked it away as quickly as if she had been burned. She silent-ly reprimanded herself for such an infantile reaction to his touch, but at the same time she folded her arms in front of her so that they would not come in contact again.

"Where are you heading with this?" the judge asked Chris.

"I am trying to show that Mr. Anderson was com-pletely broke and that he needed money badly enough to assault Mrs. Romanowski—"

Warren interrupted hotly, but keeping his voice low enough that no one else in the room could hear. "She is dealing with an issue that is outside the scope of this particular case, your Honor. John Anderson was de-nied unemployment benefits because he was convicted two years ago of a misdemeanor. That information is irrelevant to this case and would be highly prejudicial."

The judge held his glasses up and, without haste, examined the now clean lenses. Donning them once again, he dropped the gavel to the podium. "Objection sustained."

Chris stood still, anger billowing upward from deep inside of her. She turned slowly toward Warren, and her steel-gray eyes spoke more eloquently of her aversion to him and his idea of justice than words ever could have.

Walking through the glass-plated doors from the dark sidewalk, Chris clutched her leather briefcase in her hand and brushed distractedly at her peach-colored skirt. She was a raw bundle of nerves after that trying day in the courtroom. And with the closing arguments tomorrow she wondered if she would even be able to sleep tonight. But if she could just make it through this meeting tonight with an outward show of calm, everything would be all right.

Her heels clicked along the terrazzo floor as she walked down the long, empty hallway. Stopping at the office of Co-Vestment, she swung open the carved wooden door and entered.

Everyone was there already: the president of the company, the vice-president, the controller, a secretary, and Warren J. Hamilton. Chris greeted each officer of the corporation with a firm handshake. But when Warren's overpowering grasp enclosed her smaller fingers, she felt as if her bones had turned to sand.

"Good evening, Ms. Davis." His voice washed warm as wine through her system.

"Mr. Hamilton." She nodded coolly, trying to still the almost painful pounding of her heart.

"I'm sorry we had to have this meeting at night, Ms. Davis," the president said.

She pulled her eyes away from Warren's and tried to decipher what the president was saying to her.

"It was simply the only time we could all get together. You and Mr. Hamilton are tied up in court . . . the same trial, I understand."

"Yes," she and Warren answered at the same time, then glanced at each other awkwardly.

"Well, shall we get started?" the president asked, expecting no arguments. The group moved into the boardroom, and Chris felt a jolt of electricity shoot through her as Warren placed his hand on the small of her back, ushering her through the doorway.

The meeting lasted an hour and a half, with the officers of Co-Vestment falling all over themselves to convince Chris that the condominium plan was an equitable one. They had samples of financial statements, architectural drawings, mock-ups of security devices— all designed to assure her of the fact that the new condominium program would improve the quality of life for all the tenants of Willow Towers.

Chris listened quietly, interjecting a pertinent question now and then until they were finished. "The improvements you have planned are quite impressive, I have to admit," she said. "But to be quite frank with you gentlemen, these things do not interest me in the least."

The antagonistic silence that converged upon her

from around the table was so thick it could have been cut with a knife.

"What I am concerned about is the amount of money the tenants are going to have to come up with each month in order to live there. Thirty-five of the one hundred and ten tenants in the building are elderly people, gentlemen. Men and women who have worked hard all their lives in order that they might have a secure and peaceful retirement."

"Ms. Davis . . ."

Chris did not allow the president to interrupt. "Many of these people are living primarily on their Social Security benefits. They cannot afford to move to another apartment complex, nor could they find another place to live within their price range."

"Nothing is static in life, Ms. Davis," the president replied ponderously. "We have tried to be fair about this. We have held open forums with the tenants of the building, answered their questions, explained exactly what will be happening—"

"That is precisely the point!" Chris argued. "What will be happening to these people is just what they cannot accept. Yes, you have gone out of your way to provide the tenants with lovely little coffee klatches under the guise of finding an equitable solution."

"Christine." Warren placed a hand on her arm.

"Don't Christine me." She turned flashing eyes on Warren and shook her head. "Don't . . . counselor." She paused for a long moment to calm her rapid breathing. Finally she regained control and now spoke softly. "My clients, the thirty-five elderly Willow Towers tenants, are willing to fight this. Let me ask you gentlemen a question if I may. When you were considering the purchase of this building, did you have the abstract of title reviewed?"

"Of course we did," the president huffed indignantly.

"Who did the review?" Chris asked.

Everyone at the table looked at Warren for the answer.

When he answered, he appeared as calm and unflappable as always. "One of our attorneys—a specialist in real estate, I might add—reviewed the title."

"Oh," Chris smiled like a wily fox. "Perhaps you had better check again," she suggested as she inserted her legal notepad into her briefcase, snapped the lock, and stood up. "Gentlemen, my clients and I will wait with bated breath to hear what you have found in the abstract."

Warren quickly stood up also, shaking hands with the men at the table and, under the pretext of working out a last-minute solution with his adversary, hurried out into the hall after Chris.

"Christine, wait."

Her muscles tightened involuntarily as she heard the tapping approach of his shoes on the stone floor.

"You pulled a pretty good bluff in there," he chuckled. "You almost had me fooled there . . . for a minute."

"We have nothing further to discuss, Warren," Chris replied tautly.

"I just wanted to walk you to your car." He smiled as he again placed his large, bold, and warm hand against the small of her back. The imprint of his fingers seemed to burn through her blouse and into her skin. Suddenly and inexplicably she wanted to feel more, wanted to know those hands, those fingers more intimately. She was aware of a tightening need within her body, but she struggled to hold it at bay.

"Walk me to my car? That's rather old-fashioned, don't you think?" she responded sarcastically.

"I have a lot of old-fashioned ideas when it comes to you." He pushed open the door and cocked his head, smiling as she frowned up at him.

"I'll be fine. My car is over there." Warren followed the line of her vision to the small black MGA parked in the lot.

"Christine," he spoke as if to a child. "It is night, dark, late. You are downtown. The doors of your car don't even lock."

She was standing very still, watching him as intently he was watching her, trying to deny how nice it would be to have him take care of her.

He looked down at her, meaningfully. "I don't ever want you to become a statistic, Christine," he said softly, stroking her arm above the elbow. "Not you."

Chris felt the shallowness of her own breathing as she stared at Warren, searching the starlit glow of his eyes and the candid shape of his mouth. "Warren." She sighed, trying to find a way to loosen this emotional hold he had upon her. "You and I are . . . so different." She closed her eyes briefly in frustration. "Our views of life, our goals . . . we are not at all alike!"

"Christine." He slowly breathed her name into the night, and reached up with his other hand to stroke her cheek. "What does that have to do with anything?"

"It's very important to me," she answered solemnly.

"If you're waiting for Superman to come along and help you with your fight for justice and truth, you're going to be waiting an awfully long time."

80

"I can wait." She looked up at him, her jaw set at a determined angle.

"Look, if it's the trial, I . . ."

"It's the principle of the thing, Warren. Can't you see that!" Chris pulled her arms free from his grasp. She felt a burning sensation behind her eyes, and she prayed that she would not start crying in front of him. "You have no qualms about defending people who should be behind bars."

"No qualms!" Warren's voice was beginning to rise. "My job when I enter that courtroom with a client is not to express a personal opinion as to his guilt or innocence. My only responsibility is to present every defense that the law permits, and to see that the defendant is found innocent and leaves the courtroom a free man."

"And it's my job to convict," she countered angrily.

"That is where you are wrong!" Warren exploded, startling Chris into silence and complete attention. "Your job . . . counselor . . . is to see that justice is done. Period! You present the state's evidence and its witnesses, and you attempt to prove . . . prove that the defendant is guilty. If you cannot do so and the verdict is for acquittal, then justice has been served. Don't ever make the mistake of assuming that conviction and justice are the same thing."

Chris stood open-mouthed and thoroughly chastised. But she was not about to stand there and analyze his words on the spot, so she spun towards her car, rapidly walking away from him.

He caught up with her easily, walking beside her without touching her. "I told you I would walk you to

81

your car. Now I will wait until you are safely out of the parking lot, and then I'll leave for home."

Chris scooted in behind the wheel and started the engine. Warren closed the door and squatted down on his haunches, his elbows resting on the door. Chris continued to stare straight ahead.

"Christine," he said softly, "don't be blinded by your idealism, and don't let it stand in the way of a personal bond with someone . . . in the way of a relationship with me."

Chris finally turned toward Warren, her thoughts and emotions still held in check. She had never known such confusion in her entire life, and she sensed intuitively that if she didn't put a stop to Warren's pursuit of her, she would never regain her confidence and her objectivity again.

"Good night, Warren. I'll see you in court tomorrow." As she pulled the car out of the parking lot she glanced in her rearview mirror and saw him standing where she had left him, his hands thrust deeply into the pockets of his brown slacks.

The case dragged on all morning, and the jury deliberated for over five hours, but Chris knew after the first hour that she had lost the case.

She had presented the evidence as best she could, but she had watched from the beginning as the tide turned toward Warren and the defendant.

When the twelve jurors filed back into the courtroom, the electric tension was at its crest. Chris tried to slow the rapid rate of her heart by breathing slowly and deeply. Her assistant's clenched jaw was the only manifestation of his nervousness.

Chris glanced once at Warren, and felt a tremor of rage as she took note of his calm expression.

The jurors took their seats, and the judge addressed the foreman.

"Have you reached a verdict in this case?"

"Yes, Your Honor, we have," the foreman replied solemnly.

"Will you please tell the court what that verdict is?"

"Not guilty."

While euphoria flooded one side of the courtroom Chris stoically gathered up her paperwork from the prosecution table and headed up the aisle. She turned around once before letting the door close behind her and saw Warren shaking hands with several of the jurors. As if he had felt the heat from her unnerving stare, he looked up at her, his face blank, but his eyes once again searching her soul for the answer to a seemingly unanswerable question.

Chris let the door swing closed between them.

CHAPTER 5

Chris tried to lick the barbecue sauce from her fingers inconspicuously. It tasted much too good to waste on a napkin. Adam's Ribs was one of her favorite local places to eat. And, as luck would have it, it was only two blocks from her apartment building.

It was small consolation for the defeat she had suffered in court today, but it was better than eating at home, alone with her depression. Adam's was boisterous and crowded, just what she needed to buffer her from a mental rehash of the professional beating she'd taken.

After eating all the smoky links she possibly could, Chris left the restaurant and headed back toward her apartment.

It was a typical Oklahoma summer evening, warm and calm, the entire sky bathed in amber, while the slowly melting sun lingered amid stratus clouds of violet and salmon. It was much too nice an evening to go straight home, she decided. Besides, after that heavy meal, she certainly could use some exercise. So, turning south, Chris took a longer, more circuitous route back to Willow Towers.

Rounding the corner onto the street that ran parallel to her own, a flash of red metal forced its way into her peripheral vision. She turned her head and watched as a red classic Thunderbird nudged the curb across the street and parked, with shameless disregard for the rules, in a fire zone.

Before she could decide whether to turn back or drop down into the first available manhole, Warren emerged from the car and walked to the opposite door. He was wearing tan trousers, and a dark brown blazer over a white shirt added the proper amount of distinguished elegance. As the passenger door opened a slender, stockinged leg emerged. Holding on to Warren's hand, the tastefully dressed woman attached to the leg eased herself gracefully from the car.

Chris hung back in the twilight shadows of a store awning and watched them cross the street and go into a popular dinner theater. After they disappeared into the lobby, Chris realized she had been holding her breath since she had first seen the car.

Exhaling slowly, she tried to suppress the unfamiliar stab of resentful jealousy. Don't be ridiculous, she admonished herself. So the man has a date. Why shouldn't he? He's a very attractive, single man with a life of his own.

Chris thrust her hands into the front pockets of her jeans as she turned to walk back home. Besides, why should she care what he does on his own time, anyway?

She knocked on the door of an apartment on the first

floor of her building, and the door was opened a crack by a stooped, white-haired etching of what was once, if photographs never lie, a very handsome man.

"Hello, Clifford."

"Oh, Chris, it's you. Gracious." Clifford opened the door to let her in. At least once a week Chris visited him for tea and reminiscences, expressing genuine interest over the same family albums she had seen a hundred times.

"Thank you, Clifford, but I can't stay tonight. I just wanted to let you know that the meeting went fine last night. It was late when I got in, so I didn't want to disturb you."

"Then we're going to get to stay?" His soft, worn face lit up with childish expectation.

"Well, I planted the seed, and you can just bet that the officers of Co-Vestment and Warren Hamilton are not going to sleep very well tonight." Chris beamed from ear to ear. "I think we've got them, Clifford. I really think we've got them."

"Yes, well that's just grand. Are you sure you won't stay for tea?"

"I don't think so tonight. I—"

"It's already made." He smiled hopefully.

Chris smiled back with genuine affection. "Well, I suppose one cup wouldn't hurt."

It was nine o'clock when she finally stepped out of the shower after washing away the remnants of her wretched day, redeemed only by her pleasant hour with Clifford. Her hair freshly shampooed, she brushed it away from her face with her fingers, the short, wet strands curving into natural waves above her ears.

She slipped into a man-sized baggy pajama shirt and

crawled into bed, propping her head up with pillows so she could begin the novel she had been wanting to read for three months.

Fifteen minutes later the book was still open to the acknowledgments, words of gratitude lying wasted on the printed page. Chris was staring straight ahead, thinking about what she could have done differently in the case of John Anderson.

If his case had been handled by the public defender, would she have lost? Probably not, she decided bitterly. If her case load had been lighter, maybe she would have had more time to spend on coming up with new evidence against the man. But Warren's defense had been brilliant, and no matter how much evidence she submitted, he would, most likely, have won the case.

She had had such high hopes when she left law school. As naive as it now sounded even to her, she remembered how she was going to single-handedly rid the city of its crime problem. She was going to sweep away the debris of bureaucratic red tape that littered the corridors of the criminal justice system.

What had gone wrong? Why did change have to come about so slowly and why did some things never alter?

Chris rested the back of her head against the headboard and closed her eyes briefly. Maybe she needed a break from the endless backlog of cases. The state bar association convention in Oklahoma City was only a week away. That, at least, would be a change of pace from what she was doing now. Maybe after taking a few days off she would be ready to tackle the mounds of work that lay in wait for her in the office.

Her plans for the convention next week were interrupted by the harsh ringing of the doorbell. Frowning at the intrusion into her quiet evening, Chris slipped out of bed and padded in her bare feet to the closet to slip on a worn quilted robe she had bought during her first year in college. Ruffling her still wet hair with her fingers, she walked to the door.

"Good evening." Warren's voice had a lilting inflection of wonder as his gaze settled on Chris's warm, freshly scrubbed face. She stared stupidly at him as he stood in the rectangle of her doorway, unable to project the casual indifference to his presence that she wanted.

She cleared her throat awkwardly and combed flustered fingers through her wet hair. "Yes?" she asked, as if she were speaking to a door-to-door salesman. She grimaced. *God, how stupid I sound!*

Warren shifted his stance and cocked his head at her. "May I come in?"

"What for?" She frowned, still blocking his way into her apartment.

"I'd like for us to talk, Christine."

Though her eyebrows arched in dubious anticipation of that prospect, she opened the door and stepped aside, allowing Warren to enter her small studio apartment.

His eyes traveled around the room, making note of insignificant details that Chris no longer even noticed. His gaze lit on the unmade bed and lingered there for several seconds before shifting back to Chris.

"What's the matter, Warren, your lady friend wouldn't let you cash in on the date tonight?" Chris couldn't control the sarcastic remark that had been hanging on the tip of her tongue since she opened the door.

He said nothing, but again tipped his head back quizzically, a frown pulling his dark brows closer together.

"Oh, I was taking a walk after dinner," she explained with an offhanded shrug, moving away from him and toward the bar that connected the kitchen with the rest of the apartment. "I saw you going into the dinner theater."

"And?" he asked noncommittally.

She sat down and turned quickly toward him. "Did you have a good time?"

"Yes, I did, thank you." Warren drifted toward her and sat on the second barstool.

She stared down at her hands clasped tightly on the counter top. Closing her eyes and shaking her head in disgust, she muttered, "Damn. I'm sorry, Warren. I don't know what made me say that. I sound like a shrewish wife."

"It sounds nice."

Chris's eyes immediately locked with his, almost visible sparks of flashing light passing from one to the other, holding them both paralyzed in their path for several long seconds. "It was an engagement I've had planned for a long time," he said.

Breaking the bonds that pulled her toward him, Chris stepped down from the stool and took a step backward, running her hand self-consciously across her robe as she once again remembered her disheveled appearance.

She took note of the dark brown jacket and the white dress shirt that he was still wearing. His slacks were expertly cut so that the fit was not too tight nor too loose. He looked perfect. "You look very nice," she admitted grudgingly.

He smiled as his eyes raked along the length of her body. "So do you," he responded sincerely.

Chris suddenly felt naked and more unattractive than she had ever felt in her life. She looked down at her bare feet as if they reflected her entire appearance.

"Ah, Christine? Do you mind if I have something to drink?"

"Oh . . . of course," she answered with a start. "I'm afraid I'm not very good at the social amenities. What would you like?"

"Do you have any iced tea?"

She pursed her lips to conceal her smile. "Afraid I'll take advantage of you if I offer you anything stronger?"

"Are you suggesting I have something stronger?" he countered dryly.

Blushing, she quickly stepped into the kitchen and opened a cupboard. "I'll fix some tea."

Behind her, Warren smiled to himself and removed his jacket.

"The real estate expert in our office looked over that abstract again," he related in a calm voice.

"Really?" Chris appeared to be uninterested. "And what, may I ask, did he find?"

"I think we can bypass all that, Christine. What does Clifford Palmer want?"

Chris turned around with a victorious smile and held out the two glasses of tea for him to take. Sitting side by side at the bar, Chris took her time answering.

"Mr. Palmer's needs are simple," she began. "He's an old man, a widower, with very few years left to him. Of course by now you know that he owns the vacant lot next door to the building and the west twenty feet of Willow Towers happens to encroach on his property.

Which means, of course, that Co-Vestment does not have clear title to the property."

"We know, we know," Warren grumbled, taking a large gulp of tea. "How the surveyors missed that, I'll never know."

Chris smiled inwardly at the obvious superiority of her position. "Since Clifford Palmer lives in Willow Towers, and is quite happy here too, he is willing to compromise. He will sell to Co-Vestment his interest in the property as long as the thirty-five elderly tenants in this section are allowed to stay, at their present rent . . . with the normal ten-percent increase every two years, of course."

"Of course," Warren replied dryly. "Well, all I can do is talk to the officers of the corporation about it and see what they say."

"You do that, Warren." Chris immediately regretted the harsh tone of her voice.

They were both silent for several minutes while they drank their tea—Chris with her still smoldering anger over the trial, and Warren wondering how they could put it all behind them.

Chris had to fight with her gaze, which, despite her attempts at self-control, wanted to return time and time again to the front of Warren's shirt where it spread across his broad chest and shoulders.

She didn't like these feelings he evoked from her. She didn't want to forget that they were anything but courtroom adversaries. But every time she was around him, he managed to break through that professional barrier that surrounded her. She didn't want him invading her territory and breaking down her defenses.

"I'm sorry you lost your case, Christine." He took a

sip of tea, but didn't fail to miss the hard glint of suspicion that flickered in her eyes. "Oh, mind you, I'm not sorry my client got off," he went on. "But I really do wish there was some way we both could have tasted victory."

Chris took a large gulp of tea, washing down the bitter bile taste that surged into her throat, then responded in a derisive voice, "Well, as you said before, Warren, justice was served. That's all that matters, right?"

Warren was silent for a moment, then slowly took the glass from her hands and set it on the counter. Pulling her from the stool and swiveling around on his own, he drew her between the spread of his legs, wrapping his arms tightly around her waist.

Ignoring her shocked expression, he began running his fingers through her damp hair, smelling the clean, fresh scent of it. She could feel the quick rise of his breath inside his stomach and chest, and she was aware of the electrical storm of sensations that raged through her stomach where it rested against him.

"I do know one way we can both win," he breathed against her temple.

She closed her eyes briefly. *Don't fight him, Chris,* she admonished herself. *Admit for once how badly you want this man.*

His mouth moved over hers, softening, tasting, willing her to want him as badly as he wanted her. His tongue slipped along the contour of her lips, then gently dipped inside with subtle, rhythmic strokes that tempted her with a primitive pleasure still to come.

His hands were sliding over the curve of her hips,

urging her more tightly against him with gently guiding fingertips.

Her own hands had drifted upward into the hair at the back of his head, fingers weaving in and out of the dark brown strands.

She tipped her head back, her eyes closing as his mouth moved along the arch of her neck, his lips warm and persuasive against her skin.

She tried to catch her breath. "Warren." She uttered his name in a rush of breathless sound. "This is . . . wrong for me."

"No," he breathed against the base of her neck, pulling the collar of her robe off her shoulder. "This is so right, Christine. So right."

Chris's body tightened imperceptibly, and Warren looked up, his eyes chocolate pools of desire. "Christine, let yourself go. We want each other. Just let it happen."

She watched him closely, wanting so much to believe that this was truly right, but knowing inside herself that she would regret it later. He stood for so many of things she had vowed to fight against. She had to remain strong. And yet . . . she gazed at his strong and gentle face . . . it would be so nice to feel this man all around her and within her. His arms, his legs, his mouth, his hands.

She placed her palms flat against the front of his shoulders, her eyes cast down at his chest. "I can't get past this problem of principle, Warren." She sighed heavily, then looked up at him to see if he understood. "I'm fighting against everything you stand for."

Warren puffed out his cheeks and expelled a heavy breath. He placed a hand against Chris's cheek and shook his head. "You're fighting yourself, Christine." His hand slipped to the belt loop at her waist, and his fingers loosened the knot until the robe fell open to the sides. He let his eyes run slowly over her breasts and waist and thighs, covered only by the thin cotton fabric of her pajama tops. "You think that choosing to be a woman tonight with me makes you less of a lawyer. You're made up of so many parts. You can be many things. You don't have to choose just one."

"No, Warren." She shook her head, trying to dispel the seductive power he had over her. "We're adversaries. We're on opposite sides of—"

"Wrong," he interrupted softly, placing his hand against her breast. He could feel the pounding of her heart beneath his hand, and he slowly followed the rise and peak of her breast with his fingers. Her lips parted and closed several times, but she could not speak. "We're not fighting each other, Christine. We're fighting an imperfect system."

"But that's my point." She frowned, finally finding her voice. "It's imperfect because of the things you do."

"That's ridiculous!" he scoffed, both at the turn this conversation was taking and at her slanderous remark. "We're only human. The lawmakers in this country— the men and women in Congress, the judges, the lawyers—are human. They're fallible, Christine. Not perfect. But we're doing the best we can—"

"By making the judicial system more favorable to criminals than to victims? By helping people like Anderson get off scot-free?"

"Oh, for God's sake, woman!" Warren's hands dug into her sides with all the force of his emotions. "The system has to give more to the defendant than the plaintiff."

"Why? That's unfair. What about the victims?"

"Life isn't fair, Christine. It never has been. It never will be. The law is the only thing . . . the only thing in our society that is fair; that has to be fair! By giving the defendant every possible chance for acquittal, we are showing the world . . . and confirming for ourselves, that we believe in the sanctity of life, that we believe in freedom."

Chris pulled out of his grasp and walked a few feet away. "But do we believe in freedom to the point that we'll allow criminals to return to the streets, time and time again? What about the sanctity of life for the victims of this country? And by victims I mean those of us who lock our doors at night, hoping that it will be enough to protect us."

"There are problems with the system," he admitted, standing up and walking a few paces away from her. "And there are criminals who escape punishment."

Chris was watching him closely, observing the change that had come over him. He was pacing now and his hands were thrust deeply into the pockets of his slacks, a troubled gesture she had come to recognize.

"All I know," he continued. "Is that I would rather see twenty criminals get off scot-free than to have one man unjustly accused and convicted. Because if there is a flaw in our system, that is it . . . that an innocent man can be convicted of a crime he didn't commit." She saw the look of reproach in his eyes as he turned toward her. "That, Christine, is the crime."

Warren shifted uneasily, and Chris realized this was the first time she had seen him even momentarily at a loss. Having to pause to grope for words and that evasive look in his eyes were imperfections that, she had assumed, Warren didn't possess.

He reached for his coat on the couch and folded it across his arm. "I think I'll leave now. Thank you for the tea." He turned toward the door and had stopped with his hand on the doorknob when Chris finally spoke.

"Warren, I take my law practice seriously." He turned to look at her. "It's the only thing I do take seriously."

He stared at her for a long moment, his gaze penetrating the layers of flesh and bone and spirit that comprised her entire being. The look of bleak emptiness in his eyes imprinted itself on her mind, and she knew she would not forget that look for a long time.

"You're going to be a very lonely woman, Christine." He glanced away from her, running his eyes around her tiny apartment, then letting his gaze linger on the bed. Looking back at her once more, he opened the door and stepped into the hall. But his parting remark carried through the narrow aperture and echoed in the deepest part of her mind.

"I never dreamed that I'd become a lonely man."

The case against Albert Johnston had been an unusually complicated one. His small investment company was involved in the promotion and sale of fictitious parcels of land in Colorado and in obtaining unspecified securities and bonds for its clients. Not being regulated by the Securities and Exchange Commission, the company's transactions still fell under the jurisdiction of the state blue-sky law.

Chris had been gathering evidence and looking up precedents for similar prosecutions under the Oklahoma Securities Act for a week. She had taken depositions of the innocent, if gullible, investors and had filed numerous pleadings presenting the evidence that would prove her case. This time she hoped she had done her homework well enough to get a conviction. But with Warren appearing for the defense . . .

She kept playing the words he had said to her over and over in her mind. Was she a lonely woman? Was he really a lonely man? Why did she suddenly feel split in two, her dual personalities at war with each other? This was what she had dreamed of doing with her life. She had worked for seven long years, all through school, to get here. What was so wrong with devoting everything she had to doing the best job possible?

Her secretary came in with the mail, giving Chris a respite from her troubled thoughts. Twirling a pencil between her fingers, she read each letter that her secretary had already opened. On the bottom of the stack she found one marked personal. Frowning slightly at the plain envelope, she tore it open and read the short note that was inside. "I'll be staying at the Wilshire during the convention. Room 904. Call if you need anything. Warren."

The Wilshire. She should have known. With the exorbitant legal fees he charged he could afford to stay anywhere. Well, she would be staying at a small, nondescript motel a mile away from the convention center, and she had no intention of needing anything from Warren Hamilton. If she decided she needed a man that badly, she'd find one who was safe and uncomplicated. She wasn't about to subjugate her ideals to a simple physical yen for someone who was the antithesis of everything she had worked for. Throwing the pencil down in irritation, she tore the letter into tiny pieces and dropped them into the wastebasket, her subconscious mind already committing to memory the numbers *904*.

Pushing her chair back, Chris rose and carried her file down the hallway and out into the harsh sunlight of midday. The deadline for filing this pleading wasn't until tomorrow, but at least going to the clerk's office would take her mind off that infuriating man for a few minutes. *Lonely, my foot. If he thinks I'm going to fall for those scheming shyster tactics of his the way a jury does, he's got another think coming. Lonely, hah!*

Chris pushed through the glass doors of the court clerk's office and was relieved to find that she wouldn't have to wait in line for thirty minutes to file the papers. After taking care of her business, she walked back out into the courtyard that connected most of the municipal buildings. An immediate tremor quaked through her body when she saw Warren approach. He hadn't noticed her yet, and she frantically wondered if she could possibly get away before he did.

Chiding herself for having such a childish reaction, she stood where she was, watching him approach. After all she wasn't going to be able to avoid him indefinitely. The sooner they learned to get along like mature colleagues, the better off they'd be.

Chris raised herself to her full height, and donning an expression of aloof professionalism, she smiled and nodded. "Good afternoon, Warren. Nice day, isn't it?"

He stopped in front of her and stared, his spiked gaze alone dismantling the stiff cloak of reserve Chris was wearing. "Don't, Christine. Don't direct that meaningless drivel at me. Ever."

Without another word Warren walked around her and into the courthouse. Long after the door closed behind him, Chris stared straight ahead, trying to ease her pulse and breathing back to normal. *Forget him, Chris. Erase him from your mind. You don't want him, and you certainly don't need him.*

Walking once again toward her office, she felt the lie burn its searing path through her bloodstream.

CHAPTER 6

Perspiration ran down in rivulets from her temples as Chris tried to juggle her suitcase and her purse down the endless exterior balcony of the motor lodge. According to the radio in her car, the temperature in Oklahoma City was close to a hundred.

She set her bag down in front of her door and glancing at her key to make sure she had the correct number, inserted it into the lock and turned. Nothing happened. She pushed her glasses higher onto the moist bridge of her nose. She tried again, but this time the key jammed and wouldn't move to the right, left, or back out.

"Well, hi there, babycakes." Chris raised her head slowly to look at the man who was presumably talking to her. She looked behind her to see if anyone else had been the object of his greeting. She grimaced. *Nope, Chris, I guess you're babycakes.*

"Need some help there, little lady?"

"No, thank you." Chris turned back to the task at

hand and yanked hard on the key, still unable to retrieve it from the locking mechanism.

"There's kind of a trick to those things. I'm used to them by now." He swaggered over and stood beside her. "I travel a lot," he said, leaning with insufferable nonchalance against her door. "But then, you can probably tell."

Chris glanced up from her work on the door and stared at the oil-slick talker, who was fortyish, balding, and dressed in a red polyester leisure suit. "I never would have guessed."

The man bent over, pushed her hands aside, and with cocky self-assurrance pulled hard on the key. "Hm." He yanked again. Twisting it hard back and forth, he repeatedly failed to get the key out of the lock, and Chris noticed thick beads of sweat forming on his brow.

"Listen," she said. "Why don't I just call the management, and they can get me into my room."

"Good idea." The man stood panting breathlessly as he leaned against the wall. "This heat . . . it's . . . you want to use my phone?"

"Would you mind calling the desk for me? I'll just wait here with my luggage."

"Hey." His composure had returned with his steadier breathing and he patted his chest jauntily. "That's why yours truly is the top salesmen for Shiny Bowl, 'cause I know how to get the job done."

"Shiny bowl?" Chris was positive she had not heard the man correctly.

"Yea . . . we . . . ah . . . we sell toilet-bowl cleaners. Did you know that our product removes more—"

"Excuse me," Chris interrupted tactfully. "But

101

could you please make that call for me? It's just a wee bit hot out here."

"Oh . . . sure. But why don't you come in? Afraid I'll pounce on you, are you?" He chuckled loudly at his own crude joke.

Chris forced a constrained smile between clenched teeth. "I'll wait."

"Hey, no problems there." The man shrugged and went into his room, leaving the door open as he made the call. When he returned, he looked as pleased with himself as if he had just negotiated an international peace treaty.

"All taken care of, little darlin'." He dusted his hands together. "Say, are you . . . traveling . . . alone?" Once he again leaned brazenly against the wall.

"No, I have my husband and children in my suitcase," Chris replied caustically. The heat, the jammed door, and this slippery salesman were all beginning to grate like sandpaper on her nerves.

After five interminable minutes the assistant manager finally arrived and straightened out the problem, giving Chris a new key.

She pulled her bag over the threshold and turned to close the door.

"Hey," the man's glib face and body were still planted outside her door. "Maybe later we could . . ." He cocked his head toward her room, and presumably in the direction of the bed. "We could . . ."

Chris closed the door gently but firmly in his face, twisting the dead bolt and looping the chain lock in place. Shaking her head in disgust, she carried her bag over to the bed and opened it. Why did she have to put up with this nonsense? Why did any woman? She knew women who had jobs that required frequent travel, and she wondered how on earth they could stand this kind of absurd treatment.

Pulling her dresses out of the suitcase, she took them to the closet and hung them up. As she scooped her underwear and hose into her arms she heard a strange clicking noise coming from across the room. Glancing up, she watched the handle of the door that connected her room with the one next to it twist back and forth. The first flash of fear quickly subsided, and she found herself amazed that that blithering fool would have the audacity to try such a thing. Holding the clothes in her arms, she tilted her head and watched in fascination as the handle moved repeatedly up and down until, finally deciding that it wasn't going to open, the man gave up.

This is ridiculous, she decided. She wasn't about to put up with this joker next door to her for three days. She would get another room. Damn it! What a hassle this was turning out to be. In order to calm herself before calling the front desk, she threw her underwear back into her bag and walked to the sliding door, pulling back the curtains first, then stepped out onto the small balcony that overlooked the scenic panorama of the parking lot and laundry.

"Isn't this great?" Chris jumped as she heard the now irritatingly familiar voice. Pivoting to the right, she found herself face to face with the Shiny Bowl salesman. He had changed from his leisure suit to a gaudy emerald-green smoking jacket, and he lounged possessively in the one and only chair on the balcony. "We share this balcony. Isn't that great!"

Chris glared at him, furious that she should be put in such a compromising position. Was there absolutely nowhere that she could go and not have to bear his odious presence? She started to turn back into the room, but he stopped her with his not-so-surprising invitation.

"I've got a great idea. Since you and me is all alone, why don't we have a nice, cozy little dinner in my room tonight? That turn you on?"

Chris's mouth opened to discharge one of the vilest remarks she had ever thought of in her life, but her lips quickly closed with a new thought. Maybe, just maybe, this strutting turkey needs his feathers clipped a bit. Chris leaned casually against the sliding door and cocked her head. "What's your name, slick?" She affected a seductive drawl and took a special delight when she saw him flinch and straighten up in the chair.

"Ah . . . it's . . . ah . . ."

"Take all the time you need, darlin'," she said.

"Bluett. Marvin Bluett."

"Well, I'll tell you what . . . Marvin honey. You sit tight right here and I'll be back in fifteen minutes. Sound all right, sugar?"

Though Marvin's face still registered shock that this lady had accepted his invitation, he was now rubbing his hands together in anticipation. "Su—sure!"

Chris stepped through the glass door, closing and locking it behind her. As she pulled the draperies closed she waved and winked saucily at him.

As soon as the drapes were drawn she began to move fast. Grabbing her dresses off the hangers, she stuffed them haphazardly into her suitcase, then closed and locked it. She tiptoed to the door and opened it as quietly as possible. Half-dragging, half-carrying her suitcase down the stairs, she walked past the swimming pool—if something that small could be called a swimming pool—and into the lobby. Marching up to the desk, she confronted the desk clerk with a tight expression.

"I would like another room, please."

"Another room?" The young clerk looked at her as if she had asked for the keys to the safe. "Is something wrong with the one you have?"

"Everything is wrong with it," she answered angrily. "Now will you please just give me another one, preferably on the opposite side of the building?"

"But we don't have any rooms available," he shrugged. "The Oklahoma Bar Association's in town this weekend and—"

"I know about the convention," she replied testily, suddenly feeling a wave of panic attack her midsection. "Well, what about another motel? Can you find me another place?"

"As far as I know, everything in town is filled. I suppose I could try . . ."

"Yes. Would you please do that?" Chris pressed her fingers to her temples, trying to massage away the tension headache that was gnawing at her skull. While the clerk called various hotels in town Chris continually glanced at the clock above the desk, praying that her Salesman of the Year wouldn't come looking for her. She realized now what a foolhardy game she had been playing.

The clerk finally looked up from the switchboard with an I-told-you-so expression on his face. "I'm sorry, ma'am, but there's nothing in town. Everyplace is sewed up."

Chris shifted uneasily from one foot to the other.

What on earth was she going to do now? She couldn't go back to the same room, not with that jerk waiting for her in his emerald-green smoking jacket. Maybe she could call her boss, and see what he would suggest. No, Bill had brought his entire family with him, and she didn't want to bother them about something like this.

As she frantically searched her mind for a possible solution, one name popped uninvited into her head. Warren. No, she shook her head violently, disgusted with herself for even thinking of such an idea. But then . . . what else was she going to do? He did tell her if she needed anything to give him a call. But, damn, she really didn't want to need him. For anything.

Sighing with the realization that this was her only way out of an impossible situation, she asked the clerk for directions to the Wilshire. She carried her bag to the MGA, parked in the motel's parking lot, and headed with great reluctance toward Warren's hotel.

Entering the foyer of the hotel, Chris at once felt ill at ease and totally out of place. First of all busting in on Warren without warning was really rather tacky. His offer had probably been extended out of nothing more than professional courtesy. No, she had to admit, she knew that wasn't the case. But if he thought she wasn't interested, maybe he had already found another willing roommate. Surely Chris was just one of many fish in the sea for him.

The other thing that added to her sense of awkwardness was the hotel itself. With its wide marble foyer, vaulted and chandeliered ceiling, and large geyserlike fountain in the center of the lobby, it screamed class distinctions at her. It was completely out of her price range. How disgusting it seemed that Warren should be able to afford these luxury accommodations simply because he had sold his soul to his wealthy clients.

Grimacing distastefully, Chris glanced around the lobby for one last time before she carried her bag to the elevator, stepped inside, and pushed the button for the ninth floor. When the elevator stopped, her first reaction was to let it carry her back downstairs. She should not be doing this.

Propelled by something other than conscious thought, Chris stepped off the elevator, and while walking down the long, dimly-lit hallway, she debated the pros and cons of this particular course of action. What would he think when he saw her at his door? What would be his reaction?

She glanced at each doorway she passed, searching for 904. When she spotted it at the end of the hall, she stopped, shifting her suitcase to the other hand. Approaching the room slowly, she set her bag down on the carpet a few feet away. She raised her fist to knock but stopped only inches from the door's surface. She shouldn't do this. She really shouldn't. But what else was there to do?

Straightening her shoulders, she lifted her fist again. A split second before her knuckles struck the door, she drew them back. No, this was totally idiotic. Why should she subject herself to two long days and nights with a man she didn't even like? She could just go back to Tulsa and forget the convention. There would be other years.

As she started to turn away from the door it flew open. For one long, startled moment Chris and Warren stared across the threshold at each other, shock in the expression of one and dismay at her stupidity in the face of the other.

Warren was dressed in gray pinstripe slacks, a white dress shirt, and rust-colored tie. His suit coat was draped casually over his left arm. His dark hair was neatly combed, and the touch of silvery gray at his temples lent an elegant, mature aura that both excited and intimidated Chris. It was funny, but two long days and nights with Warren suddenly didn't seem so horrible after all.

"Chris?" Warren finally broke the silence and tipped his head. When she didn't answer, he looked down at the doorknob. "Were you peeking through my key-hole?" he laughed.

Oh, damn. Chris frowned. What on earth was she going to do now? It was certainly too late to make her escape. She would simply have to make the best of this. Well, here goes . . .

"Hello, Warren," Chris tried to smile. "I'm sorry for barging in. You were leaving, weren't you?"

He glanced at the coat thrown over his arm and shrugged. "I was going to meet some guys for dinner, but that's all right. Come in."

She glanced over at her suitcase and his eyes followed her line of vision. He quickly looked back at her.

"I've got a bit of a problem," she said uneasily.

He watched her closely for a moment, then stepped out into the hall and picked up her bag, ushering her into the room.

When the door closed, he draped his coat over the back of a chair, and Chris thought she detected a certain self-consciousness in his movements.

"I don't have a hotel room, Warren."

"You didn't make a reservation?" he asked stiffly, and she could tell he was uncertain whether to make the first friendly overture or not.

"Yes, but the only room available in this town is . . . unsuitable."

"What do you mean?"

Chris sighed and began relating the events of the last hour and a half. When she had finished, Warren's eyes were flashing with amusement.

"Are you kidding me?" He laughed. "And you didn't want to have dinner with him? Just think of all you could have learned about cleaning your toilet."

"Very funny, Warren." Chris tried to scowl, but felt her mouth turning up at the corners.

Warren walked over and wrapped his arms around her waist, not a trace of self-consciousness remaining. "Just kidding. But I am grateful the guy made such an obnoxious nuisance of himself. It brought you here."

Chris loosened his hold and stepped back, clearing her throat. "Warren, look, I don't want to be any trouble. If it's not convenient . . . I mean I just need a place to sleep, and . . ."

"Sleep?" Chris's eyes jumped to his face, and she was struck by the fiery question that blazed from the depths of his eyes. She watched with fascination as his mouth curved upward in a subtle smile. "But of course, Chris." He grinned slyly. "You're more than welcome to . . . sleep here."

Tearing her eyes away from him, Chris was suddenly all business. "I'll sleep on your couch, and I'll pay for half the room, and . . . well, we can talk more about it later. I don't want to keep you from your dinner date.

109

I think I'll just unpack a couple of dresses and hang them up if it's all right."

"Why don't you come to dinner with me?" He leaned against the wall beside the closet.

"I thought you were having dinner with some other men?"

"It's just some old lawyer friends I've known forever. Nothing formal. You might find it interesting. Besides, you have to eat."

"Oh, Warren, I don't want to barge in on—"

"You won't be barging in on anything." He grasped her upper arms gently and turned her around to face him. "I'd like it very much if you came."

Her lips parted in silent refusal as she stared up at this man she had such ambivalent feelings about. She wanted to dislike him, knew she should, but whenever she looked at him and felt his steady brown eyes boring into her, her feelings of animosity vanished in the sultry air around them.

She watched him leaning down toward her, his eyes trained on her lips, his own lips parting as they moved toward the soft flesh of hers. It was a gentle kiss, softly compelling, appealing to all that was warm and womanly in her.

She felt her skin come alive with tingling, electric impulses, and a radiant glow suffused her body. His hands were still holding her arms, tangible proof that he would not wrap them around her and try to overpower her with his strength. It was unnecessary. She was totally devastated by the quiet dominance of his mouth on hers.

When he released the pressure and looked down at her, his gaze drifted from her eyes, washed so soft and gray in the dim light of the room, to her mouth, still moist and sensitive from his kiss.

When he spoke, his deep voice faltered with husky indecision. "If we're going to dinner tonight, I guess . . . we'd better go."

Chris's answer came out in a rush of breathlessness. "I'm not dressed for dinner."

"I can wait. There's really no hurry. They were going to have drinks in the bar first anyway."

"Are you sure? I mean about wanting me to come?"

He squeezed her arms gently before releasing her. "I'm sure." To relieve the awkwardness of the moment Warren lifted her suitcase onto the bench at the end of the bed, then went into the bathroom to make room on the counter for her things.

Chris smiled in surprise when she looked up through the doorway and noticed Warren shoving his shaver, brushes, shampoo, and toothpaste to one corner of the counter. He was acting as unsure of himself as an overly excited teenager with a girl in his room for the first time. But surely once or twice before in his forty years he had shared a hotel room with a woman!

While she showered, wayward thoughts kept tumbling through her mind. What was Warren doing in the other room? What if he were to come in here with her? What if she were to ask him to? Desire and bewilderment intersected in a jumble of sensations that she had never known before.

After Chris dried off and slipped into a soft apricot linen dress, her high heels lifting her forehead to the level of Warren's mouth, she was ready to go. The appreciative look in his eyes made her very glad she had brought along something besides her customary business suits to wear.

Together they left the room and took the elevator downstairs to join Warren's friends.

"There he is." A man who seemed to be as round and soft-hearted as a peach rose from a table in the bar and clapped Warren on the back. The other three men greeted him jovially. "We were wondering what happened to you." Their eyes shifted to Chris and made a slow, appreciative appraisal. "I think I see now why you were late."

The other men at the table readily agreed, and Warren smiled and placed his hand on Chris's rigid back. "I'd like to introduce Christine Davis. She's with the D.A.'s office in Tulsa."

"Chris," she corrected as she shook hands with a couple of the men.

"In what capacity?" A middle-aged man stood up and extended his hand toward her.

"I'm a prosecutor," Chris replied in precise, even tones.

She caught the troubled flicker in Warren's eyes. But what did he expect her to say? Why should she let them assume that she was some secretary with whom he was having a casual affair?

After Chris had shaken hands with each of them, they all sat down and ordered drinks for Warren and Chris.

Sipping her wine slowly, she listened to the talk that drifted easily around the table. These men were at ease with each other; that much was obvious. Warren explained that he had gone to school with two of them, and the rest had known each other professionally for years.

"This is our annual get-together," one of the men explained to Chris.

"Actually," Warren whispered, "we have a sort of sibling rivalry going on among us. Every year we exchange stories to see who's accomplished the most."

Everyone laughed easily, and Chris tried her best to join in. This kind of socializing was so difficult for her. She would like very much to have a group of friends with whom she could interact this way. But she actually knew very few female attorneys, and she couldn't seem to establish the same kind of rapport with the male lawyers she knew. Even in law school it had been extremely difficult to establish a rapport with any of her fellow classmates. She watched in frustration for three years as the men grew closer together, walking out of the classroom discussing both a legal technicality and that night's party in the same breath.

With Chris, relationships had been an either/or situation—either she socialized with her friends who were not lawyers or she established an aloof and strictly professional relationship with her colleagues. She had come to accept this way of thinking as the right way. But sitting with these men and listening to their ready banter about both social and legal subjects, Chris was acutely aware of her self-imposed isolation.

After they drifted into the elegant hotel restaurant for dinner, Chris found herself receding more and more into the cool detachment on which she had come to rely to get her through these encounters.

"Chris, where are you staying?" a lawyer from a small town east of Oklahoma City asked.

"Oh, well . . . ah, I'm staying here at the Wilshire."
She had to concentrate on not looking at Warren.

"They must have really improved the salary for
prosecutors since I was one." He laughed, and Chris
smiled tightly. Was that all these men thought about—
money?

She couldn't resist the obvious retort. "The point of
working for the D.A.'s office is not to make a lot of
money."

Warren's mouth quirked sideways in an expression
that was more indulgence than irritation. But from
there the evening moved steadily downhill.

Chris withdrew into herself, listening as politely as
she could manage, yet offering very little to the conver-
sations. She felt a chasm opening up between Warren
and her, and she knew from the way his jaw tightened
every few minutes that he was aware of it also. It had
always been there, Chris reminded herself. And they
had both been fooling themselves to think that they
could simply choose to overlook the vast differences
that existed between them.

When they returned to the room at last, the silence
between them was palpable as Warren removed his suit
jacket and hung it in the closet. Chris walked slowly
about the room, avoiding eye contact at all costs.

"Christine—"

"What!" she answered, too defensively.

Warren looked up sharply, catching her eyes for the
first time since entering the room.

"Look, I'm sorry if I ruined your evening with the
boys," she blurted out impulsively.

"It was meant to be your evening as well as mine. I

114

wanted some good friends of mine to have a chance to meet you."

"Well, I'm sure they were delighted," she sneered. "We had so much in common."

"You do have a lot in common with them," he growled. "If you'd just let yourself go for one goddamn minute."

"Oh, well, next time I'll put a rose in my teeth and dance on the tables."

Warren grabbed her upper arms, but this time there was no gentleness in his touch. "Why can't you just act like a woman, Christine? Why do you always act like you're going to knock the balls off the first man who tries to get behind that tightass veneer you wear?"

Chris glared at Warren and pulled away from him angrily. Kicking her shoes off, she picked them up and threw them in the closet.

"You just don't understand, do you? You have no idea what it's like for a woman in my position. It's so easy for you, since you don't have the same commitment to the law that I do."

"And pray tell, what is *my* commitment to?" His arms were folded in front of him, and his mouth was hard and forbidding.

She waved her arm to encompass the room. "Well, I'd say it's money . . . and status and . . . it certainly doesn't seem to have anything to do with any basic principles."

"Just because I don't get on my soapbox every ten minutes like you do does not mean I don't have any principles." He shook his head in frustration. "I just happen to get tired of talking about law all the time. There are other things in life, you know. And sometimes when I'm with a beautiful woman, I like to steer away from shoptalk." He sighed heavily. "Christine." He spoke her name softly and gently this time. "Can't we discuss—"

"It's easier for you, Warren." Chris had stooped down to organize the shoes she had thrown in the closet. "You can interact socially with other attorneys without the relationship appearing to be on a—"

"On a what?"

"Well, on a physical level . . . a sexual level." Chris stood up but kept her back to him, busying herself with straightening the hangers in the closet. She jumped when she felt Warren's large hands on her shoulders, his strong, tender fingers kneading the back of her neck.

"Are you trying to tell me that every time you talk to a man it turns into a sexual relationship?"

Chris smiled sheepishly at the ludicrous question.

Warren turned her around so she was facing him. His hands ran up and down her arms, loosening the rigidly clenched muscles of her body. "You must be a very promiscuous woman, if that is the case," he whispered with a teasing smile.

Chris turned her eyes toward his, silently pleading with him to understand how difficult it was for her to combine her professional and personal interests.

"You're a beautiful woman, Christine. But you must learn that any kind of professional work requires fellowship. Joking, personal relationships, informal discussions of outside interests . . . these are all a part of it. And—" He pulled her up tightly against him so that she could feel every powerful contour of his body. "You must learn that you can free that beautiful woman who is inside you and still be a professional."

Chris did not look up at his face, mesmerized instead by the rapid rise and fall of his chest. "A personal relationship with you in other words." She spoke softly, afraid to know the answer, yet wanting more than anything to hear the words.

"That's right, Christine." His voice rustled like a warm breeze across her scalp, intimate and enticing. "A very personal relationship with me."

She glanced up, and her gaze was captured by the mastery and the sexual power of his eyes. The warm brown centers held her in their dark embrace, making love to her with their directness, allowing a small glimpse inside this man's thoughts, a foretaste of the untold pleasure that he could give her.

As her conscious thoughts were lost in this winding maze of sensual sensations Warren evoked in her, Chris's hands went up to his arms, gliding upward, her fingers straining to reach inside the fabric of his shirt as they trailed upward to his neck. She let them slip into the hair at the back of his head, grabbing a handful of the thick, dark strands and holding tight.

"You win, counselor," she whispered. "Tonight I'll be a woman with you."

With a low satisfied moan Warren removed her glasses and tossed them onto the desk. He pulled her tightly against him as his mouth took possession of her parted lips, passion surging into her mouth as his tongue swept inside, tasting and probing for all the deep secrets that lay locked within her.

She held his head tightly, not wanting to lose that mouth, that elemental blaze, for even a moment. God she wanted this man! And she had wanted him since the first night she ever saw him. Tonight she would forget the animosities, the differences in philosophy. Tonight she would let the woman inside her breathe and come to life.

"I've wanted you so badly, Christine," he murmured against her throat as he trailed warm, moist kisses up and down the sensitive flesh of her neck.

"Whatever you want, Warren," she breathed, and it sounded almost like a plea. "Anything." Pressing her pelvis tightly against his, she delighted in his sharp intake of breath.

Warren's hand was lowering the zipper at the back of her dress, and he pulled the material off one shoulder, kissing the tender spot he had exposed. "I want it all, Christine. Every square inch of you."

As her knees began to buckle, Warren scooped her into his arms and carried her to the wide, waiting bed, sitting down on the edge with her in his lap. He lowered her to the covers, her hips still pressed against his pelvis and his lips trailing across the top of her dress. She wanted to feel his mouth on her bare skin, and with the material of her dress as a barrier, his kisses became sweet torture.

Her own hands were set loose in a torrent of exploration, traveling along the crisp texture of his shirt, slipping in between the buttons to touch the firm, warm flesh beneath.

Lifting her slightly, Warren pulled the dress off her shoulders and arms, lowering it to her waist. The only barrier that remained was the thin nylon camisole that covered her chest. His hand moved slowly across her covered breasts, stroking them gently and reverently with his fingers. Cupping one breast in his strong hand, he lowered his head and took the tip in his mouth, the silky material of her bare camisole now wet and slick across the surface of her skin.

She felt as if she would explode from the need she felt for him. Running her hand down across the front of his slacks, Chris tentatively explored the masculine demand that strained to meet her hand.

He covered her half-clothed body with his own, gently opening her legs with his knee. As he pressed his pelvis against her arching body, his mouth opened over hers once again, taking possession with his tongue.

The vigorous ring of the telephone on the bedside table tore through the veil of passion that wrapped the hungering night around them. Warren's tongue continued its pursuit of something deep within her mouth, and Chris's hands never ceased their wanderings across his hips, dipping down between his thighs.

The phone intersected the sounds of passion again and again. "No," Warren moaned into her mouth. "No. Don't stop, Christine. Don't . . ."

The insistent ringing refused to be ignored. "Damn!" Warren reached for the receiver and lifted it off its cradle, slamming it onto the bedside table. His lips never left hers except to travel down her neck and across her cheek and ear before returning once again to taste the sweetness of her mouth.

"Warren! Warren, are you there?" The voice split the air in two. "Warren?"

With a groan of frustration Warren raised the upper part of his torso just enough to allow him to reach for the phone. "Hello!" he growled, his voice hoarse and ragged in the night. "Yes . . . oh, hello, Ben. No . . . no, I wasn't asleep."

Warren sat up, pulling Chris back onto his lap, and

shaking his head ruefully at the interruption. His mouth dipped down to her neck, his tongue blazing a heated trail across her skin.

She didn't stop the wanderings of her hands. Her fingers moved to the front of his slacks, sliding the zipper down with an exquisitely slow precision.

Warren watched her as he held the phone to his ear, and he closed his eyes when she wrapped her fingers around him so intimately.

"Hang on a second." He held the phone away from his face, covering the mouthpiece with his hand while he brought his ragged breath under control.

He sighed wearily into the phone. "When was the arrest, Ben?"

Chris's eyes opened wide, a knotted thread of foreboding unraveling through her bloodstream. An arrest. A case.

Warren expelled another deep breath as he glanced down at Chris with longing. While he listened to his partner on the other end of the line for a few moments, Chris sat up beside him, her hand held firmly in check. His gaze narrowed and shifted abruptly to Chris, and she felt the swift tensing of his body—a tightening that had nothing to do with passion. "Who's prosecuting this one?" he asked grimly.

Chris immediately bolted away from his side. She was on her knees on the bed, trying to calm the harsh rattle of her breathing. A client was under arrest, that's what he was talking about. A case her office was handling. A case she herself might be in charge of.

She looked at Warren, but he had his back turned to her as he spoke brusquely into the receiver. "Tell him not to say anything, Ben. Not a damn word to anyone.

120

Let Walter handle it until I get back, but I want it understood that no deals are to be made with the D.Á. until I'm there. Right. No, it's . . . okay, Ben. No, I was just . . . reading. Yea, good night." Warren replaced the receiver with meticulous care, as if he were afraid of what was waiting for him when the call ended. He turned slowly toward Chris, who was climbing off the bed.

"Christine?" He stood and walked around the bed toward her, reaching out with a hand to touch her cheek.

She turned her head to avoid his touch. "This was a mistake, Warren." She tried to fit her arms into the sleeves of her dress, but she was shaking so badly from the physical and emotional strain of almost knowing the feel and taste and warmth of Warren's body that she couldn't even dress herself. "It never should have happened," she said, swallowing the lump of tears that tried to force its way upward.

"That's not true, Christine." Warren reached for her waist, not allowing her to escape from his grasp again. "We have to learn to deal with these professional intrusions into our personal life together, that's all."

"We are not going to learn to deal with anything. I can't do this. I cannot divide myself in two this way. The minute you got that phone call, I felt all the animosity toward you coming back." She stopped when she saw the pain, like the last flicker of a dying ember, flashing in the center of his eyes.

He stared at her impassively for a few seconds, then nodded wearily. His eyes trailed down her body, lifting up again to her breasts, still covered by the thin camisole. His eyes remained transfixed there for an agoniz-

121

ing moment before he reached for her dress and helped her slip it back up over her arms and shoulders. Turning her around, he pulled the zipper up to the top.

At the same time Chris felt a tremor of longing so deep and painful that she wanted to beg Warren to assuage the need, to ravage her body and rid her of this shell she wore. But she didn't. She let the zipper rise to a stop, then remained tense when he placed his hands on her shoulders from behind.

"Christine . . ." She waited with bated breath for him to speak, but the words she wanted to hear never came. "I'm going to go out for a while. I'll see you in the morning." He refastened his slacks, grabbed his jacket from the hanger in the closet, and walked out the door.

It closed so quietly behind him that the sound could not be heard across the room. Yet, in Chris's mind, it had the unmistakable dragging sound of a cell door closing, locking the world and all its infinite pleasures out, and leaving Chris dreadfully alone within the moldering walls of her solitary prison.

CHAPTER 7

Their eyes collided and flared with the explosive force of a new dawn across the packed auditorium. Chris quickly averted her gaze, removing her glasses and wiping them on a tissue with infinitely slow strokes. But when she placed them firmly across the bridge of her nose and stole another furtive glance in his direction, Warren was still watching her steadily.

She sighed heavily and shifted her eyes back to the guest speaker. Though she was paying only scant attention to the man at the podium, her boss, sitting next to her, appeared to be devouring every word. Why was she having so much trouble keeping her mind on what was being said? The subject matter of the seminar was of great interest to her, and it was one she had been looking forward to especially, yet her thoughts were as disordered this morning as tangled coils of wire.

She had not slept well in the least, and when she woke up at seven o'clock this morning, the first thing her eyes lit on was Warren's powerful frame sprawled inertly across the couch. She had lain awake for interminable hours last night, wondering where he had gone and when he would return to the room. She had finally fallen into an uneven sleep and didn't wake when he slipped in during the still hours of the morning.

Sitting up in bed after the phone rang with her wake-up call, Chris had been intrigued—no, mesmerized—by the sight of his muscular frame stretched out full length, fully clothed, along the small couch. His coffee-colored hair was tousled and several wayward locks fell across his forehead, and his cheeks and chin were covered with a fine, dark shadow. His suit coat had been thrown carelessly across the back of a chair and his wrinkled white shirt was open to the waist, revealing a tanned, broad chest tapering down to a trim waist.

Chris jumped in her chair when laughter suddenly broke out in the auditorium, spinning her thoughts around in a one hundred and eighty degree revolution. Flicking her eyes around self-consciously, she realized that the speaker no doubt had made a humorous remark, so she smiled without the faintest clue as to what had been said. Her gaze shifted to Warren, and her mouth and jaw tightened automatically when she noticed him laughing easily along with everyone else in the room.

Why wasn't he as tired as she was? Why wasn't he miserable too?

Trying to focus her thoughts on the matter at hand, but completely failing to do so, Chris was relieved when the seminar was finally over. As everyone stood up and stretched their cramped limbs, she turned to make conversation with Bill, but was utterly dismayed when she heard Warren's name springing from his lips, followed by a hearty greeting.

"Warren. Great to see you." The two men exchanged powerful handshakes and slapped each other's broad shoulders with what appeared to be genuine affection.

"Hello, Bill. Sorry I had to stand you up last Sunday on the golf course."

Chris listened to the friendly male prattle with growing irritation. How could two men who were constantly at odds in their professions be such close friends?

"Morning, Ms. Davis." Warren turned to include her and nodded perfunctorily.

"Mr. Hamilton," she responded in a tight voice.

"Where are you staying, Warren?" Chris heard Bill ask.

"At the Wilshire. How about you? Did you bring your family?"

Bill chuckled lightly. "Yes. The kids have been bugging me all summer to go somewhere, so here we are. Big deal, right?"

"And you, Ms. Davis?" Warren turned toward her with a demonic gleam in his eye. "Where are you staying?"

Her answering look was stony. "With a friend."

"How nice. That must be fun for you."

"Delightful," she sneered, not catching the surprised look in Bill's eyes as he listened to the icy repartee between the two attorneys.

With a mental shrug Bill picked his jacket off the back of the seat, brushing at an invisible speck of lint. "Well, if I'm going to catch this next seminar, I'd better be going. Coming, Chris?"

"No, I don't think so. I'll see you tomorrow, Bill."

"Okay. So long, Warren. Give me a call when you get back home. Margaret's been wanting to have you over for dinner."

"Sounds good. Give the family my love."

"I'll do that. Bye, Chris," Bill said, as he moved up the aisle and out into the crowded hallway.

Chris picked up her blank legal pad and turned toward the exit.

Warren quickly caught up with her rapid pace. "Are you going back to the hotel?"

"I'm going for a walk," she responded coolly.

"Good, I'll walk with you."

Chris stopped and turned toward Warren. "Look, Warren. I'm sorry that this—this arrangement is not working out. I'm going to walk for a little while, then I'm going to get my things out of your hotel room and drive back to Tulsa."

"But the convention isn't over until tomorrow.".

She sighed. "I know, I know. But I'm not getting much out of it and besides . . . you shouldn't have to sleep on the couch."

"Okay, you can sleep on the couch tonight." Chris glanced at him sharply and caught the mischievous grin that played around his mouth and eyes.

She couldn't control the hint of a smile that lifted the corners of her mouth. She didn't want this chasm between them. She wanted their parting at least to be civil. Self-consciously she looked down at the slim wedge of space between them. "It's more than that, Warren, and you know it."

"I know."

Chris peered up again and her eyes locked with his.

126

He was the first to smile, a tender, understanding smile that swept her once again into the subtle embrace of his charm.

"Come on, let's walk." He took her hand in his and led her out into the bright sunlit day. The landscape around them was endlessly flat, the barren, sunburnt earth relieved only by the towering thrust of glass and steel.

This day, like the one before it, was hot and dry; even the branches of the trees hung limply, as if all sap had been extracted from them. Chris adjusted the collar of her white cotton blouse in a unconscious effort to allow what little air was stirring to circulate against her skin.

They walked in the opposite direction of the hotel, neither one of them in any apparent hurry to get back to the room.

"What are you going to do over Labor Day?" Warren asked, and Chris realized with a smile that he was making a supreme effort to conduct a friendly, safe conversation.

"My family lives in Norman, so I thought I'd go visit them," she answered. "It's been a while since I've been there."

"Any brothers or sisters?"

"A brother and a sister," she said. "Both younger. My brother's a sophomore at the university, and my sister graduated last spring and just got married a month ago. Her husband has a job waiting in Colorado, so they'll soon be leaving."

"What made you choose law?" It was a simple enough question, and he had been merely curious. But he also had to have been aware of the abrupt change in

Chris's expression when he asked the seemingly innocuous question.

Chris had felt the tension ebbing away as she talked casually about her family. But now a shutter dropped down over her eyes. Warren was treading on more personal ground, the realm of the past and present that comprised who and what Chris Davis was, a dividing line that she did not want crossed.

"It's as good a profession as any other," she mumbled vaguely.

She was aware of Warren's acute gaze piercing the carefully sculpted layers of her expression, attempting to grasp the thoughts that she was keeping under such close guard.

"And you?" she countered, hoping that by pivoting the conversation around to him, his interest in her life would wane.

"I grew up in Tulsa," he began easily, but Chris could tell by his smile that he was onto her trick. "My grandparents were among the original settlers of Oklahoma Territory. After Oklahoma Territory and Indian Territory were combined into a state, they migrated farther east, ending up in Broken Arrow. I was an only child . . ."

She nodded with unkind complacency, as if that alone accounted for his self-indulgent egotism.

Happily oblivious to her assessment of him, Warren continued. "In college I majored in history, and law seemed like the logical progression from that."

"So, in other words," she said accusingly, "you had no commitment to law from the beginning."

Warren's eyebrows arched sharply as he looked

down at her cynically. "Well, Christine, we can't all be as noble as you are."

She swallowed hard and made a wry face as his words fell like sharp, slashing blows. She had to admit that had been a very stupid thing to say. Stupid and pompous.

"Sorry," she murmured, her downcast face contrite, and tired from all her efforts to simulate detachment. When were these personal arguments between them going to end? she wondered wearily. Would they always remain so far apart?

"Truce?" Warren held out his hand, and she slowly extended hers, letting him wrap it tightly in the warmth of his fingers.

She wished it could be as easy as this—walking through life hand in hand. But she knew it wasn't. Nothing was easy. Nothing was simple or clear-cut. Too often, she had learned since becoming a lawyer, life's values were negotiable and up for sale, stretched and twisted and tinted with obscure shades of gray until nothing made sense to anyone anymore.

As he sensed the tenor of her troubled thoughts even without knowing their content, Warren squeezed her hand affectionately. "Are you ready for some air conditioning?"

Chris pulled her clinging blouse away from her skin and groaned laughingly. "This answer your question?"

Backtracking quickly, they headed in the direction of the hotel, eager to get out from under the devouring sun.

They approached the final block to the hotel, and without thinking, Chris blindly stepped off the curb, only to be abruptly jerked back by Warren's hands.

"Chris, for God's sake, be careful!" She felt the blood drain from her face as a streak of shiny blue metal sped menacingly through the intersection. She hadn't seen the car coming, hadn't been aware of any danger, but if she had stepped even one foot farther into the street, she would surely have been run down.

As she inhaled sharply Warren wrapped his left arm around her waist, holding her tight against his side. It took several seconds for the blood to seep back into her face and until she was breathing evenly again.

"Be careful," he whispered again, and she felt the blood bounding against her skin as his thumb brushed lazily against the side of her breast.

After they crossed the street safely, and continued the last block to the hotel, Chris tried to still the thudding of her heart enough to speak. "Warren, may I ask you something?"

He frowned when he saw the downturned curve of her mouth. "Anything."

"Well, I was just wondering what it is exactly that you see in me." She hurried ahead with her question before he could reply. "I mean I know I'm not the love of your life or anything, but I think you're attracted to . . . to me." She looked up at him questioningly, a pink flush staining her cheeks.

"Some feelings are hard to define." He smiled slowly, the corners of his mouth lifting with each new thought that came to him. "I don't know, Christine. I like women who are intelligent, who have principles . . ."

Chris shifted her gaze to his face and saw that he was watching her steadily, honestly. No hidden meanings lurked in the shadows of his brown eyes.

"Yes, even an unscrupulous old shyster like me likes someone with a conscience and a sense of duty." He grinned and winked at her. "I also know you're very beautiful and soft, and you should never underestimate what you mean to another person."

Chris watched him closely, trying to decipher the cryptic meaning of his words; wanting to follow this elusive vein wherever it led. What did he mean by underestimating herself? What was he trying to say to her? She felt as if she were trapped and lost in the twists and turns of this dialogue like a scuttling mouse in a maze. Was she being overly optimistic, searching for some fulfilling morsel of cheese at the other end, or was she still trying to avoid the path to fulfillment for fear of some vague but fatal trap that she could not predict?

Warren stopped walking, but didn't loosen the grip of his arm around her waist. He gazed down at her, and his eyes held such honest, hopeful need that she felt the bones in her knees turn to water. "Don't go back to Tulsa tonight," he implored. "Stay . . . please. I won't do anything that you don't want me to do, Christine."

Her lips parted, but the words stayed inside her. *How can I say no to you, Warren?* she cried inwardly. *How can I keep from wanting you?*

He continued to watch her until she was able to answer. "All right, Warren. I'll stay." She watched his deep sigh of relief, and his thumb once again lifted up to stroke the swell of her breast. They continued walking, but this time their steps were quicker, more urgent, as if both were unconsciously heading toward that same elusive moment in time when they would at last be able to satisfy their deepest needs.

They strode together across the parking lot, heading

131

in the direction of the front door. When they passed Warren's car, Chris glanced over, out of habit, toward hers to make sure the sides had not been dented or marred by an inconsiderate car door. She frowned and looked in another direction. How stupid of her to have forgotten where she had parked it! She stopped, and Warren, still holding her waist, stopped with her. She swiveled her head around, scanning every corner of the parking lot for her car.

She slipped free of Warren's arm and walked up and down several rows, glancing right and left. Nothing.

"Christine, what's the matter?" Warren followed a few paces behind in confusion.

"My car." She looked at him in bewilderment. "It's gone."

"Gone!" Frowning, he too began scanning the parking lot for the small black MGA.

"It was parked right here." Chris pointed to the space now occupied by a sleek, silver Mercedes. "I know it was right here. Right here, Warren!"

Sensing the panic that was beginning to rise in her, he forcefully grabbed her arm. "Christine, just calm down. We'll find it."

"But it was right here!"

"I know. I know." He held on to her hand tightly. "Let's just take our time and look around carefully."

They began walking up and down each row, covering the entire parking lot before they returned to the spot where Chris was positive she had left the car. They went around again, looking everywhere, hoping that somehow she had been mistaken as to where she left it. Again there was no sign of the car.

"It's gone, Warren." Chris leaned against the hood

of the Mercedes, defeat etched in the harried lines of her face. "My car is gone."

Warren wasn't about to accept defeat yet, so he dragged her with him into the lobby of the hotel and up to the front desk.

"I want to see the manager," he ordered.

"I'm sorry, sir, but the manager is out."

"Then the assistant manager. Whoever is in charge."

"Well." The desk clerk looked uncertain. "I am, sir."

"This woman's car is missing. It was parked in your parking lot."

"Missing? From our lot?" The desk clerk dropped the pen he was holding and looked as if he too were about to panic. "Are you sure?"

"We're sure," Chris replied dully. "It was there when I left this morning to go to the convention hall and now it's gone."

"There is a silver Mercedes parked out there." At this point, Warren squeezed his eyes shut in thought. "License number ST 4386. Does it belong to one of your guests?"

"Well, I don't know. I—"

"Look on your room registration forms. You always get the license number. See if you have it listed."

The clerk fumbled through the room registrations, pulling out one card after another in search of that particular number. "Yes, here is it." The clerk clutched the card to his chest. "But I don't think we're supposed to give out that sort of information."

"Look," Warren said harshly, rapidly losing patience. "All we want to do is talk to the owner. See if he or she saw anything unusual when pulling into the lot."

133

"Well, I suppose it would be all right," the clerk hedged. "But, why don't I call and ask them about it first. If they want to talk more, they can come down."

Warren expelled an exasperated sigh. "Fine. Just call."

Chris leaned against the counter wearily, shaking her head now and then over the very real possibility that her car had been stolen. How could it have happened? And in broad daylight?

The clerk returned from the phone, stating that the owner of the silver Mercedes had seen nothing. When he had pulled into the lot, the space was empty. "He says he's sorry he can't help, but he really didn't see anything."

"Okay." Warren shrugged; he had not really expected to get any pertinent information from that source but felt he had to try anyway. "Call the police, will you?"

"Sure," the clerk responded, "I'll do that right away. Why don't you two wait in the coffee shop, and when the police get here, I'll send them in."

"Thank you," both Chris and Warren answered as he took her hand and led her toward the coffee shop. They found a booth near the front entrance where they could keep an eye on the lobby for the police.

"Two cups of coffee," Warren told the waitress when Chris didn't respond to her presence.

"No," she broke in quickly. "Iced tea for me, please. Damn!" she muttered after the waitress left, letting her face fall into her hands. "I feel like somebody just died."

Warren reached over silently and took both of her

hands in his, rubbing his thumbs across the backs of them.

"Isn't that stupid," she cursed herself. "I mean, to get that attached to something like an old car."

"Not at all," he replied honestly, and she was grateful for his calm strength at this moment. What would she have done if he hadn't been here to face up to this with her?

After almost an hour two police officers finally appeared and Chris showed them several times exactly where she had parked the car.

"Are you a guest in the hotel, ma'am?"

"Yes . . . I mean no." She glanced awkwardly at Warren.

"I'm a guest in the hotel. Ms. Davis is staying with me."

The two officers exchanged furtive glances before jotting down the information on their note pads. After they went back into the hotel to talk in the cool of the manager's office, Chris gave them a detailed description of the car. "It should be easy to find. It's fairly unique. There aren't too many of them around anymore."

The officers shifted uneasily before one of them spoke. "All the more reason why you shouldn't expect to get it back, ma'am. No one in his right mind is going to drive a stolen car like that around. It will probably be stripped and the parts sold separately. I'm sorry we can't be more optimistic, but those are the facts of life."

Warren wrapped his arm around Chris's shoulder, offering a silent brand of condolence. Looking at it realistically, Chris knew the policemen were right. It would be foolish for a thief to drive a car like that around town. Still, she couldn't yet give up all hope of finding it.

"Well, at least I have insurance," she said ruefully as she and Warren took the elevator back up to the room.

Warren frowned. "Don't count on it, Chris. Insurance companies don't understand the value of classic cars and they rarely pay what they're worth." He hesitated before adding, "If there is anything I can do in the meantime . . . What I mean is, if you need some . . . financial help with another car . . ."

"I don't need any help," she snapped, then immediately regretted her tone of voice. "Thank you, but I'll manage fine."

They reached the room, and Warren extracted the key from his pocket. Opening the door, Chris walked in and immediately dropped on the couch in limp exhaustion. Warren tossed the key on the desk, then pulled back the curtains and the sliding door that opened onto the balcony.

A fragrant breath of fresh air filtered into the room, and Chris leaned her head back against the sofa, breathing deeply to purify her thoughts.

"Looks like it's going to rain," Warren commented as he stepped out onto the balcony. From her spot on the couch Chris watched him standing there, gazing out over the lush hotel garden that defied the rust-red dirt from which it sprang.

Night was falling fast and for several minutes neither of them spoke as they watched the transition from day to evening. Night never fell in the summer until about nine o'clock, but with the heavy cumulonimbus clouds that were billowing in from the west the sky was already shading into darkness.

Warren was standing at the railing, looking down into the garden when Chris, after first removing her glasses and setting them down on the desk, got up from the couch and walked out to him. Placing a tentative hand against his back, she began hesitantly.

"I want to thank you for what you did today, Warren. It meant a great deal having your help and . . . and having someone to share the burden."

Warren pulled her into the circle of his arms, her back pressed tightly against his chest and his chin resting on the top of her head. "Everybody needs a shoulder now and then," he said, and Chris detected an unfamiliar note of vulnerability in his voice.

For what reason could you possibly need a shoulder, Warren? Chris's mind balked at this startling concept. You are the most self-sufficient person I know. What could you need that you don't already have?

She quietly voiced the doubt. "Surely not you."

Warren turned her around, still holding her in the tight enclosure of his arms, but with her stomach and breasts and pelvis pressed against his hard body. His breath accelerated with the closeness of her, and Chris detected a sudden quickening of his heartbeat, so near her face.

"You have no idea what you're saying, Christine. I need things that I can't even define. I need companionship, I need someone to share my problems, I need . . ." Warren's eyes captured her and held her imprisoned in their dark intensity. "I need you, Christine. I really need you."

The words and the voice and the feel of his arms enclosing her melted through the tough fiber that had surrounded her for so long. She knew that this was

137

what she wanted, what she had always wanted. To be a part of this man, and to let her flesh meld with his.

Slowly she lifted her hands to his face, tracing the sharp line of his jaw, softening it with the tips of her fingers. She let them glide across his face and his closed eyes as her hands passed his brow and moved into the hair at his temples.

Warren's hands fanned out against her back, fingers trailing lazily down her spine and onto her hips. The breeze brought by the clouds brushed against their faces and rustled lightly through their hair.

The darkening sky softened their features as they moved closer, their lips almost touching but prolonging the moment of exquisite torture. When their mouths met, their lips were already parted, and their tongues collided with a burst of longing so intense that Chris felt her knees buckling underneath her. It was a kiss of night, of promise, of passion yet to come, and she savored and delighted in the taste of him.

His tongue began a long, slow foray around her still parted lips, from corner to corner before moving on to stroke her teeth. Her own tongue reached up to meet his, and together they rolled and pulled and sipped at the sweetness that lay within them both. He kissed her hungrily, intoxicating her with his own drunken passion.

Warren pulled back, holding her face between his hands, his eyes devouring her features with an intensity that was overwhelming. "I want you Christine, but not just in the physical sense. I want your friendship and your strength and your beauty and your softness and . . ."

Chris stood up on tiptoes, closing off his words with

her mouth. As she drew herself up her body slid like butter against his torso, and she felt his need in the hardness of his contours, in the pounding of his heart, and in the rapid, uneven rise and fall of his chest.

Loosening the buttons of her simple blue shirtwaist dress, he pulled the fabric over one shoulder and worshiped the now exposed skin with his mouth.

Scooping her up in his arms, Warren carried her through the door and into the room, setting her down gently on the wide bed that waited for them. The door was left open, and the night breathed gently upon them, whispering words of encouragement and love that neither of them could find the breath to say.

Pulling the dress gently from her body, he then slowly removed every trace of clothing they were wearing. Dropping down beside her, he placed feather-light kisses from her chin to her navel, returning time and time again to her breasts, where his mouth grew ravenous and insistent.

She could see, even in the dark, the boldness of his body, and she wanted him within her now more than anything she had ever wanted in her life.

Lifting up on one elbow, Warren's hand traced a leisurely trail across her skin, beginning at her throat and wandering with seeming aimlessness across her breast, arousing her by degrees with each stroke, moving down across her stomach. His fingers moved slowly between her thighs and found her wanting him and ready, as he wanted her.

Adjusting his weight over hers, he parted her thighs with his knee and thrust gently into her, lifting her hips with his outstretched fingers to meet him pulse for pulse. The wind shifted and blew a light spray of rain into the room, but they were unaware of it.

At last, lying side by side, they felt the cool mist that whirled like flecks of shimmering light through the velvety darkness.

Warren raised up again on an elbow and gazed down lovingly at the woman beside him. He entwined one leg with hers and brushed away the droplets of moisture that clung to her forehead. "You are beautiful, Christine." His eyes traveled down her body with wonderment before returning to her face. "You're what I have waited forty years to find."

Chris lifted a limp hand to his chest, her fingers rustling through the soft hair that trailed down his chest and abdomen. "Can we make this work between us, Warren?" Her voice was soft and silvery, like tiny drops of rain that nourished an already overflowing pool of love.

"Do you want to make it work, Christine?" His fingers trailed silkily across her breast, circling and arousing an unquenchable desire.

Chris closed her eyes briefly while his hand played across her skin. When she opened them, he was watching her closely, studying the desires that hovered just under the surface. His eyes were dark and fathomless, but she knew what lay behind them. She could see and feel his need and his love for her.

"Yes, Warren. More than anything in the world, I want it to work."

His mouth lowered over hers once again, and he watched with fascination as her lips parted to receive whatever he could give her.

CHAPTER 8

Warren pulled out Chris's suitcase again, set it down on the ground, then turned his suitcase sideways in the trunk. Lifting hers back up, he tried once again to fit them both into the cramped confines of the luggage compartment.

Chris leaned nonchalantly against the side of the car, trying to hide her amused grin. Only moments before she had tried to offer a suggestion, but Warren had cut her off with an impatient wave of his hand.

He glanced up and caught her grin, then moved in front of her, leaning over her in playful menace. "What are you smirking about?"

"I just think it's funny that a man as brilliant as you are in the courtroom can't seem to fit two small suitcases into the trunk of a car."

"Funny, huh?" He pressed her against the side of the car with his body, and she felt the familiar tightening in her abdomen and a sensual heat rising in waves between them. "Well, counselor." His low, rich tones vibrated along her cheek. "If you're so smart, why don't you do it?"

"I thought you'd never ask," she replied with a superior tilt of her head.

When Warren stepped back to release her, Chris walked around the rear of the car and studied the capacity of the trunk, her hands perched purposefully on her waist. After a minute she glanced complacently at Warren, then quickly began to shift the bags around until they fit snugly side by side in the trunk. Dusting her hands together with satisfaction, she couldn't control a giggle at Warren's disconcerted expression.

"So what?" He feigned indifference as he closed the lid of the trunk.

Chris laughed outright and scooted into the passenger seat.

Though she was still terribly upset about the loss of the MGA, she felt an uncommon thrill over this chance to ride home with Warren. She knew, even before the odometer began to tick off the miles, that the drive and the time they spent together were going to be much too short.

"What did you think of the convention?" he asked after they were heading north on the Turner Turnpike.

"What convention?" She smiled provocatively as she leaned her head back against the seat and peered sideways at him.

He glanced at her and smiled crookedly, reaching over to rest his right hand on her thigh. "I wish you wouldn't look at me like that when I'm driving."

"Like what?" she asked coyly, aware of subtle electrical impulses that darted along her nerves as his fingers stroked lightly against the inside of her thigh.

"Damn." He squeezed her leg tightly. "You're a sadistic little thing."

Trying to relieve the sexual tension that stretched taut between them, Chris flipped on the radio, tuning it to an easy-listening station.

Warren frowned and reached over to switch it to an AM talk show. "I detest elevator music."

Chris stared mutinously at him. "Well, I hate these blabbering call-in programs."

They glared at each other for a long moment, weighing the strength of each proposition. Warren was the first to back down.

"Well, if you have to listen to music, please find something that doesn't remind me of sitting in a dentist's office, okay?"

Chris fumbled with the dial until she found a hard rock station. Smiling impertinently, she leaned back against the seat, not failing to catch the narrow-eyed glare Warren directed at her.

While Warren drove, Chris dozed in her seat, and she was dreamily aware when he pulled her head over against his shoulder, wrapping his right arm around her waist. His hand traced a slow pattern on her stomach and breast, and she knew, even in her half-awakened state, that by doing this he was torturing himself as much as her. But it was an exquisite torture that neither of them wanted to end—not just yet.

As soon as they crossed the city limits of Tulsa, Chris was wide awake. Warren took the Skelly Drive exit east, then turned south on Lewis Avenue.

"This isn't the way to my apartment, Warren."

"I know. It's the way to my house."

Chris's breath was suspended while she waited for him to explain.

"I thought we would go fix a home-cooked meal. I've got some steaks that are begging to be grilled."

She laughed. "I'm sure. But I do have to work tomorrow, you know."

"You have to eat, too." He smiled enticingly at her and she felt her knees weaken with a hunger that had nothing to do with food.

He continued to drive out Lewis Ave, past Oral Roberts University, past the new housing additions that seemed to spring up overnight.

"I didn't know you lived in the country."

He grimaced. "It used to be. But the way the city is growing, it'll be in the heart of town before long."

Finally turning off the avenue, Warren drove down a curving blacktop road for a half a mile, then turned onto a dirt drive, passing through an open gate. As the road wound through the trees Chris became more and more excited to see how this man lived. She knew so little about him, and yet she felt as if she had known him all her life.

As he pulled into the circular drive Chris got her first glimpse of the house. Low and rambling, the exterior was faced with natural stone and cedar. Two stone chimneys protruded from each end of the house. The bedding plants and trees around the house had an overgrown, almost unkempt appearance. It gave the impression that Warren so desperately wanted privacy and seclusion that he had allowed the plants to take over, hiding much of the facade from view.

She glanced at the man beside her. What was he

hiding from? she wondered. What was behind his own facade that he wanted to conceal from the world?

Warren had already climbed out of the car and opened the trunk, pulling the suitcases out. When she noticed her bag in his hand, he shrugged sheepishly. "Just in case."

She couldn't control the trembling that seized her body as she watched him carrying her suitcase toward his house.

He bypassed the front door and walked around to the side. "I never use the front door," he said as he opened the side door for her.

She stepped into a rustic den, a feeling of warmth immediately wrapping around her and drawing her into the security of the room. The walls were paneled with a deep brown wood and the oak floor was polished to a high sheen. One large Indian rug dominated the floor between the leather couch and wing-back chairs. Hanging unpretentiously on the walls were some of the great masterpieces of western art—Remingtons and Russells, Indian paintings by Tiger and West. Priceless western bronze figures served unobtrusively as book-ends on the shelves.

Chris knew how much money was tied up in this room, and yet there was no sense of pretense in the decor. Everything was understated, refined, to express a masculine elegance that reflected Warren's own character.

"Its beautiful, Warren." Chris smiled, and he set the bags down and reached for her hand. Pulling her toward him, he grasped the back of her head and lowered his mouth to hers.

"I've been waiting all day to do this," he murmured

as his mouth moved over her parted lips, lovingly entreating as his tongue circled her lips and then her teeth, patiently finding the center of her mouth.

When her arms lifted to his shoulders, the pressure increased and they were both aware of the need that circled around them.

Warren raised his head and touched her cheek softly. "I guess I'd better show you the rest of the house, or we may never get beyond this room."

He picked up the suitcases, and Chris tried to steady her pulse as she followed him into the foyer and living room. As she looked around this room, she could see why he avoided using the front door. It was elegantly furnished but cold, and she knew beyond a shadow of a doubt that he spent little time in it. There were no personal mementoes, no warm colors, nothing that looked or felt like Warren had been here.

He didn't stop in the living room but continued through the foyer toward the back of the house. From the front door Chris could see that the back wall was entirely made of glass so that all the rooms on that side of the house overlooked the woods behind it. They passed the country kitchen on the left and the small attached breakfast room behind it, also with a glass wall that opened onto the woods.

Across from the kitchen and between the living room and dining room was a strangely incongruous room that contrasted sharply with the elegance of the two rooms that flanked it.

"This is the original log cabin that was here," Warren explained as Chris walked with fascination into a room that was used as a pub and game room. "The rest of the house was built around it."

"Did you build this?" she asked, thoroughly impressed with the creative inspiration behind it.

"No, I bought it about five years ago. The log cabin was built at the turn of the century. Don't look too closely, 'cause you'll probably find all sorts of things living in the corners."

He was right. Chris noticed a tall green plant protruding through a crack in one corner, straining to survive in the dim light.

"My housekeeper would love to come in here with a machete and chop all the plants down, but it's the one room in which I let nature have its way."

Chris looked at Warren with fascination. She could imagine him coming home from the office at night, sitting down at the table there with a beer among the wild plants, letting the tension of the day drain out of him. She had a sudden irrational jealousy for this house, this room that he came home to each evening, the den that insulated him and made him feel secure.

"Listen, I've got to go put these bags down or my arms are going to be six feet long." Warren walked back into the foyer and Chris followed with a new sense of understanding. He really wasn't so tough and formidable. He was only a man—a man who was vulnerable and who needed a peaceful refuge to return to each night to help set the world right.

She stepped behind him into his bedroom with a sense of trepidation. It was as if she were intruding into a domain where she did not belong but where she wanted, right now, more than anything to be. The same masculine colors that dominated the den and pub were evident here. It was a room where Warren felt comfortable, where he belonged. Chris glanced unwittingly at the bed and her eyes lingered. The wide four-poster was covered with a soft brown spread, and she could not keep her mind from picturing Warren stretched across its length, the sheets draped casually over his naked torso.

When she at last looked up, she saw that he was watching her closely, and she felt a frightening surge of longing for this man. She had never felt this way before in her life. Nothing had prepared her for this all-consuming ache of sweet pain. It was an exhilarating yet frightening feeling that she no longer wanted to remain alone in her ivory tower. She would rather slay her dragons from within the protective enclosure of Warren's arms.

He closed the space between them, but only to wrap his arm around her shoulder and lead her to the kitchen. "Let's fix some dinner," he suggested lightly, but she could tell by the quick rise and fall of his chest that the suggestion had not come easily.

"I've got some steaks in here somewhere." He began rummaging around in the freezer, finally pulling out a foil-wrapped package.

Chris placed her hands on her hips. "Maybe you're not as hungry as I am, but I don't think I can wait five hours for those to thaw."

Warren held up his hand to silence her. "The miracle of contemporary technology to the rescue." He smiled as he unwrapped the foil from the steaks and tossed them into the microwave, setting the dial to Defrost and pushing the button.

"How disgustingly modern." Chris feigned boredom with twentieth-century technology and leaned back against the counter with her arms crossed in front of her.

"True, but still an indispensable gadget to have around. Okay, here are some potatoes." He began tossing them over to her from where he was standing by the refrigerator. While Chris scrubbed the potatoes Warren set the table and uncorked the wine. When the steaks were thawed and the potatoes took their place in the microwave, he tossed them on the indoor grill and Chris fixed a salad.

She glanced at the trendy cooking devices around his kitchen and chuckled. "For a man who lets plants grow through the walls of his house, this kitchen is certainly an anomaly. Which is the real you?"

He looked as if he had never thought of it before. "I guess they both are." He glanced at her, his eyes narrowed in careful scrutiny. "Look at you. You drive a twenty-five-year-old classic car, but you live in a high-rise apartment building. Talk about incongruities."

Chris turned back to the salad fixings with a frown. "Drove a classic car."

Warren expelled a slow breath, angry at himself for bringing up the subject. "How are you going to get to work until you get another car?" he asked softly, treading gently around her abused feelings.

"Well, I was thinking about that. A friend in my building works downtown, so I'll ask if I can ride with her."

"I'd be happy to pick you up if . . ."

"No." She smiled and shook her head. "Our schedules are too different. I'll just ride with her." She looked up at Warren standing over the grill and smiled. "But thank you for the offer."

149

He reached over and stroked her cheek, the gleam in his eyes sparkling under the fluorescent lights. "Anytime."

They devoured the steak, potatoes, and salad, and sipped at a fine Bordeaux while they ate in companionable silence.

When they were almost finished, Warren finally broke the quiet. "Why did you close up on me yesterday when I asked about your reasons for getting into law?"

Chris set her fork down on her plate and clasped her hands under her chin in a thoughtful pose. "Yesterday the question seemed like an intrusion."

"And today?"

She smiled and set her plate aside, clasping her hands once again on the table in front of her.

"When I was a sophomore in college, I still wasn't sure what my major should be. I jumped around from one thing to another." She fell silent and stared at her hands for a long moment. "My grandparents lived in a suburb of Oklahoma City, an older, run-down area . . . but their home for many years. One night a gang of kids broke into their house, stole everything they could carry, tied my grandmother to a kitchen chair, and beat up my grandfather." She shook her head sadly and looked up at Warren as he reached over to cover her hands with his.

"The kids were caught and brought to trial." She sniffed bitterly. "But the case was thrown out on a technicality."

"Were your grandparents all right?"

"Oh, yes," Chris shrugged. "They survived it all with a kind of resignation that I never could accept. So

. . . now you understand the basis of my noble commitment to the law . . . revenge."

Warren frowned and shook his head. "I don't believe that for one minute. Don't forget I've watched you in the courtroom, Chris. You're not motivated by revenge."

She sighed heavily. "I suppose not anymore. But that was my reason for switching to pre-law in my junior year."

"And very understandable too," Warren concluded, weaving his fingers between hers and squeezing gently.

A moment of silence passed between them. "That's why the elderly tenants at Willow Towers mean so much to you, isn't it?"

Chris looked at Warren, who was watching her so closely, and nodded. "Yes, it is." She took another sip of wine before changing the subject.

"May I ask you a professional question now, Warren?" Chris even surprised herself with the request. It seemed odd that she could ask the opinion of a man she had thought of only a few short days ago as her most formidable adversary.

Warren's eyes, too, held a hint of surprise at the request. But the momentary shock quickly gave way to a soft glow of gratitude. He had not expected her to trust him so much already. "Sure, what is it?"

"Well, I have a case where I feel pretty confident I can get a conviction. I'm sure I have enough evidence to put this guy away for a long, long time. But there's a slight problem. The arresting officer neglected to read him his rights."

"You're in trouble," Warren concluded taking a sip of his wine. "Case closed."

"Well, not necessarily." A troubled frown creased her brow. "You see, the public defender—brand-new, I might add and still wet behind the ears—doesn't know about it."

"How can that be?"

"Because the defendant doesn't even realize it. I was told in confidence by someone on the police force. My problem is whether to divulge that information." She glanced up, looking miserable.

"Christine, don't be ridiculous!" Warren exploded. "Hell, no, don't tell anyone."

"But I talk about justice all the time, and it just seems like I'm . . . I don't know, corrupting it or something."

"Christine, your principles are admirable. But you have to realize that your responsibility . . . your only responsibility is to the state. Your job is to prosecute. It's the defender's job to defend. It's up to him to ferret out all the information he can to help his client. If there's something he doesn't know, that's his tough luck."

"I suppose you're right," she conceded, still troubled by what seemed to her a deception.

"Of course I'm right," he responded with complete self-assuredness, taking another healthy swig of his wine. "Your responsibility is to the state."

"You sound more like a prosecutor than a defense attorney." She smiled, shaking her head in wonderment over Warren's ability to see both sides objectively.

He lowered his glass slowly, and she was suddenly struck by the strange glaze in his eyes. His jaw had tightened, and he held the glass between his fingers as if he wanted to squeeze it until it broke. When he didn't look back at her, a sharp sliver of alarm wormed its way up to her brain. What had she said to provoke such an impenetrable response from him?

As dinner ended and the dishes were cleared away the taut silence relaxed into easy conversation once again. Chris washed the dishes while Warren put them in the dishwasher, and she quickly forgot about his peculiar reaction to her remark and clung instead to the closeness that grew with every minute between them.

Looping the towel over a rod in the lower cabinet, Chris stood up and noticed Warren leaning back against the counter, his hands lightly holding the edge. Sensing the invitation in his eyes, she moved close to him, clasping her hands behind his neck. "That was a wonderful dinner." She smiled softly.

He gazed down at her lovingly, then slowly moved his hands around to her hips, pulling her up tightly against him, his feet spread so that her body fit perfectly between his thighs.

"How about dessert?"

"What did you have in mind?" she tilted her head back, exposing the creamy white flesh of her neck.

"Oh, maybe a little of this." His mouth dipped down to nibble the base of her throat. "And this." His tongue circled her ear. "You're not fattening, are you?" He grinned against her cheek as his hand reached up to stroke the swell of her breast.

She moaned deep in her throat as his mouth once again trailed in a silken line across her neck. "No, strictly low-cal."

"Good," he growled. "Then I think I'll have you after every meal." Their mouths met and caressed.

"And before every meal." Their lips opened and closed in sensuous delight. "And during every . . ."

Their parted lips came together in drunken rapture, an all-consuming, inflaming passion that swept them headlong into the smiling, breathless night, where arms and thighs and mouths and hearts converged, entwined, and became one.

Chris lifted the fine crystal glass to her lips and took a small sip of her water. Once again her eyes traveled around the room in awe. It was such an elegant restaurant, and she couldn't for the life of her figure out why the senior partner of Warren's firm had invited her here for lunch.

She was aware, as she had been since they had sat down, that Benjamin Doddson was watching her closely, so she smiled courteously at him.

"This is very nice," she said, hiding her self-consciousness very well.

Ben Doddson glanced around the room as if he were seeing it for the first time, then shrugged. "Yes, I suppose it is." He leaned back in his chair, his glass of scotch held suspended only inches from his mouth.

"I'm sorry Warren couldn't be with us today. He had to go out to Bartlesville to take depositions." Ben stared thoughtfully into his glass. "I suppose we could have waited for him, but . . ." He peered over the rim of the glass at Chris. "Well, I decided I would pursue you on my own. You know . . . Warren says you're really hot stuff, Chris." The drink finally reached his lips and he took a fastidious sip of scotch.

Chris hands jerked in her lap. What on earth did Mr. Doddson mean by that? What did Warren mean?

"I've been wanting to get over to the courthouse to catch your act, but the timing has been all wrong."

Chris breathed a sigh of relief. He was talking about her law practice of course, and Warren must have been referring to her ability as an attorney. She picked up her glass of water and took another drink, and this time her smile was natural and relaxed.

The silverware and the glasses in the restaurant blended into a tinkling background of affluent music, and the realization slipped into Chris's mind that this kind of professional socializing wasn't so bad after all.

"What are your career goals?" he suddenly asked, and the question hung for several minutes in the air while the waiter set their plates down in front of them. Chris had ordered an asparagus crepe, and the delicious aroma made her realize how hungry she was.

"Well, actually I haven't thought about it too much," she answered truthfully, after picking up her fork to cut off a bite of crepe. "I've been with the D.A.'s office for less than a year, and I hope I'll be there for quite some time."

Ben Doddson, still leaning back casually in his chair, shifted the glass to his right hand and took a slow drink before setting it down beside his plate. Chris watched him, trying to anticipate his next question. Suddenly she was feeling very uneasy, as if there were some ulterior motive behind his lunch invitation after all. She chewed and swallowed mechanically, no longer aware of the delicious food in front of her.

"To be quite frank with you, Chris, we're always on the lookout for bright young additions to our firm. Warren is constantly bringing your name up around the office, and so, I decided it was time we met."

Chris frowned as she picked up another bite of crepe. An addition to his firm? She tried to laugh lightly. "Of course, I do work for the opposition."

Benjamin Doddson shrugged. "People switch sides all the time, you know."

Chris felt an ominous chill scurry down her spine. Why were they having this discussion? What had Warren been saying around the office? Surely he wouldn't . . .

"What do you say, Chris? We could sure use you on our team."

Chris looked at the smug expression on Mr. Doddson's face, as if he expected with absolute certainty that she would jump excitedly at this opportunity.

"Mr. Doddson, I'm . . . flattered by your offer," Chris nearly choked on the lie. "I mean . . . I presume it is an offer?"

The other attorney nodded with philanthropic humility. He cleared his throat before continuing in a soft, conspiratorial voice. "Of course, we would expect a certain amount of reciprocity on some of the cases that are pending between us. You know, a little quid pro quo. For example, Chris"—Ben failed to notice her drawn features as he spoke—"this investment broker, Albert Johnston, who's being so callously treated by your office, happens to be a very good friend of mine."

"In other words, Mr. Doddson," Chris said between tight lips, "if I want to join your firm, I would be expected to exchange something for something, perhaps plea-bargain on this case . . . or were you wanting me to drop the charges altogether?" she finished sarcastically.

Benjamin Doddson's face tightened noticeably in re-

sponse to her tone of voice. "I'm talking about cooperation, a professional courtesy. You do understand reciprocity, don't you? I mean, I assumed that Warren had
softened you up a little to this arrangement."

"Softened me . . ." The words stuck in Chris's throat.
Warren was supposed to have softened her up! Oh, my
God! The fork dropped to her plate with a clatter.
Warren says you're really hot stuff. The words threaded
through her mind with new meaning. Warren had been
softening her up so that she would agree to . . . to what?
To join their firm, or had the offer been made only so
she would feel pressure to drop the charges against
their good friend Albert Johnston. *You're really hot
stuff.* What had Warren told everyone about them?
Why would he have done this to her? She thought he
cared. She thought he loved her!

Chris put her napkin down gently on the table. Too
gently. The forces that were raging inside her were
straining to break the bonds of control in which she
held them.

"Mr. Doddson." Chris clutched the edge of the table
with her fingertips. "I have no idea what Warren has
told you about me, but whatever it was, the fact remains that I have no intention whatsoever of leaving
my post with the D.A.'s office, nor will I even consider
reducing the charge against Albert Johnston. He is a
criminal, and he will be tried as a criminal."

She reached for her purse and stood up, glaring at
Doddson for one last time. "And I consider this
. . . this bribe . . . this quid pro quo garbage of yours
and Warren's to be loathsome and vulgar and . . .
criminal."

Chris walked out of the restaurant, Ben Doddson's

157

stunned expression following her dignified stride every step of the way.

Once outside, her dignity gave way to indignation. And along with her anger emerged a hurt so powerful, so painful, that it seemed to rip upward through her abdomen, tearing at the finely woven dream she had wrapped around herself. She had exchanged her ivory tower of personal noninvolvement and high-minded ideals for Warren's love. Now she knew what a dangerous crime of passion that had been.

To be sure, she would now have to pay the price.

CHAPTER 9

The feelings lay deep in the darkness within her, festering, blistering. The wounds were exposed and raw, and she couldn't find the salve that would heal them.

She knew she couldn't face Warren, even though she realized that avoiding him was the coward's solution. But that couldn't be helped. She could not see him. The hurt was too fresh, too exposed, and she would not give him the privilege of examining that hurt within her. He was too good at probing, too careful an observer not to see what he had done to her. God, but she detested him.

All week she avoided his calls and managed, by some turn of luck, not to intersect his path in the winding corridors of their profession. Luck, hah! The word itself was a blasphemy. Luck was something she had run out of a long time ago. Warren had ripped it, body and soul, from her life.

Knowing that the best remedy for her pain was work, Chris delved into it with a vengeance. Legal precedents, statutes, gray-tinged interpretations, inconsistencies in testimony, admissible and inadmissible evidence, plea bargains and indictments all blended into a kaleidoscopic whirl of duty and obligation. Yet all clarity was gone, along with all focus and direction. Chris blinded herself to anything beyond the task that lay in front of her at any given moment.

It was a jarring shock when she finally had to face Warren as she had known all along she would have to do.

His face was gray—like everything else in her world these days—as he leaned over her desk after closing the door to her office. His eyes searched her face for the reason behind her return to isolationism.

"Is it because Doddson took you to lunch?" His voice sounded unnaturally high. "Is it because he made a stupid mistake in trying to bribe you? Surely that's not why you're avoiding me, Christine."

Impressed, despite the hurt she was feeling, that he could go immediately to the heart of the matter, Chris remained poker faced.

"You obviously thought I could be bribed." She had finally gotten the words out, and was astounded at how natural her voice sounded. *And you thought you didn't have a flair for drama, Chris. You're outstanding!*

"I had nothing to do with that."

"Really." She raised her eyebrows dubiously.

"Christine, Johnston is a friend of Ben's. It's understandable that he would want to help his friend."

"He offered me a job with your firm, you know. On your recommendation, of course." Every word came out dripping with sarcasm.

Warren stared at her stonily for a few moments.

"You flatter yourself a little too much, Christine, if you think that I would have had anything to do with that."

All the color suddenly drained from her face as she considered the implications of this. *Was* she flattering herself? Perhaps she had been right. Maybe Doddson had offered her the position only with the intention of having her drop the charges against his friend. She had assumed that it had been Warren's idea all along. But then Warren had said she was hot stuff, had been talking about her around the office. And it had been his job to soften her up to the idea. Priming her for the coup de grâce, she decided in a fit of self-pity.

At that moment a knock on the door signaled the end of one round, sending both Warren and Chris retreating to opposite sides of the ring.

"Come in," Chris said when she was safely ensconced in an emotionally neutral corner.

The secretary entered and smiled weakly at the man she knew to be the infamous Warren J. Hamilton. Handing a file to Chris, she explained her interruption. "This just came up, Chris. The arrest was made this afternoon. Bill said to get it to you, pronto. Says there has to be an immediate indictment or . . ." She glanced awkwardly at Warren's sullen back as he stared broodingly down at the courtyard below. "Well," she began again in a hushed voice. "He wants us to have our position prepared before anything leaks to the press."

"Okay, Joan." Chris flipped open the file, mentally dismissing the secretary from her mind even before she had left the room. Warren was another problem altogether. She had to figure out a way of getting him out of her office. If she didn't have to look at him . . . If she wasn't confronted with those polished brown eyes, that persuasive mouth. . . .

Something in the file caught her attention and she reread the sentence three times before the meaning was apparent. The man who had been arrested this afternoon and charged with the murder of a sixteen-year-old boy had been arrested once before. At that time he was indicted for attempted murder, first-degree assault, second-degree assault, and possession of an unlicensed gun. He was acquitted on all four counts. The attorney for the defense—Warren J. Hamilton.

Something fierce and violent bubbled up from the depths of her mind, rendering Chris incapable of speech for several moments. Warren had turned back to face her, but she no longer saw his face, or his eyes, or that mouth. She saw only evil, saw only the face of a murderer who had taken the life of a sixteen-year-old boy.

"Congratulations, Warren," she said suddenly, her voice like a deadly whisper.

Warren was taken aback by her tone, but he said nothing, waiting to see what had set her off this time.

"You should be very proud of yourself," she hissed in the same low tones. "You earned a sizable fee the first time around, I'm sure. I wonder how much blood money you'll get this time?"

"What are you talking about?" He was no longer trying to hide his bewilderment.

"The name Fred Zimmerman mean anything to you?" she said scathingly.

His mind was blank for a moment, and suddenly she saw the recognition flash across his eyes.

"I see you do remember," she said, turning the file around slowly so that he could read it for himself.

Warren kept looking at Chris for a long moment before he lowered his eyes to the paper in front of him. He read a few lines, and then his eyes went blank. He was still looking down, but Chris knew he was no longer seeing the words. Finally, slowly, he raised his head and stared at her.

To anyone else the expression in his eyes would have seemed impassive, but to Chris they were filled with a pain so intense that her own hurt dwindled into insignificance. She knew, without his saying a word, that she had broken the final thread of love that they had woven between them. She had thrown a devastating mistake in his face, had virtually accused him of complicity in this appalling crime, and she had proven that she did not at all understand the imperfections of man.

As he turned and walked from the office, closing the door behind him, Chris knew that this time the barely audible click of the latch had the finality of a death sentence.

The days and nights blended together into an indistinct present. Life moved onward, marching through long, hot days when the sun beat down relentlessly, baking the red ground beneath it to a hard, cracked crust, through summer storms when the sky blackened and washed away the brittle soil, leaving thick, tarry gumbo the color of burnt umber for the sun to once again bake dry.

Chris continued with her work. After all, it was all she had. The Fred Zimmerman case consumed much of her time, as did the trial of Albert Johnston. Warren had handed both cases over to other members of his firm, and Chris was greatly relieved to find that she would not have to meet him day after day on the tense battlefield of the courtroom. And yet she missed seeing his face. She missed the playful war of wills that had blazed between them for a while. She missed him—more than she ever could have imagined. But she had accused and convicted him without a trial, and she knew he would never forgive her.

When the media was finally tossed a few crumbs on the Zimmerman case, it was simply to announce that the defendant had been indicted for murder in the first degree. Regardless of whether the ultimate penalty would be carried out if the defendant were found guilty, the indictment at least satisfied the public's desperate craving for justice.

The trial of Albert Johnston was a long and harrowing one, and Chris returned to her apartment every night with fatigue wrapped like thick layers of fat around her bones and muscles. Aside from the technical difficulties involved in proving that a stock swindle had taken place, the case impinged too closely on Chris's personal life. Though certainly not responsible for the problems between Warren and her, it had arisen at the wrong moment, smack dab in the middle of their tenuous peace treaty, much as a land mine left from the previous war might explode with a force that could damage both sides irreparably.

Beyond the fact that the defendant deserved to be punished and his conviction was another favorable mark on Chris's professional tally, she received very little satisfaction from winning a conviction in the trial of Albert Johnston. She wondered what Warren would think of her now.

She continued to wonder, and then one day she received her answer. On an overcast day in October, Chris strode into the clerk's office with a pleading in hand. The sky was the color of weathered cedar, uniformly dull except for small darker pockets of moisture. Her gray suit blended perfectly with the day, and the yellow silk blouse she wore under her jacket hinted at a sunny disposition that wasn't there.

She pushed through the heavy plate-glass doors and they closed slowly behind her with a thirsty, sucking sound. Deciding to get a little exercise, she opted for the stairs rather than the elevator, but it was a decidedly poor choice.

As she lifted her feet to climb the three flights she heard descending shoes clapping against the tiled steps. Glancing up, she was stopped short by the tall figure moving in her direction. When Warren looked up, he too stopped, their eyes locking in a tightly controlled stare, each holding in whatever thoughts were bubbling inside them.

Chris held her breath and felt the blood surging into her heart, a painful pounding beneath her rib cage that drummed incessantly in her ears. With each passing second the tension mounted, and her left hand as it rested on the slick banister grew wetter and clammier.

At last he made the first move, stepping carefully and gingerly, quietly placing one foot on each stair as he drew closer to her. When they were only a hairsbreadth apart he stopped, but only for a moment this time, while his eyes searched Chris's expression for a glimmer of . . . of what? What did he want? she wondered.

What did he hope to find? Her eyes closed briefly when he moved on past her, following the hallway out into the joyless gray day.

At the next floor Chris took the elevator, too weary to continue on foot.

It was during a rather uneventful day when Chris had managed, with no small effort, to wedge Warren to the back of her mind for a little while that she literally stumbled across a new and startling piece of the Warren Hamilton puzzle.

She had been working on a case that would come to trial in about three months and had been researching past cases that were essentially similar. Since her secretary was indisposed—and did not normally consider the procurement of coffee as one of her duties—Chris walked down the hall to the machine. She usually preferred tea, but today she felt the need for something stronger, something that would prod her awake when she felt like collapsing onto the mountainous stack of files she was reviewing.

Walking back to her office, she tripped over a tall stack of legal files that was piled calf-high beside her desk. The coffee in her cup sloshed over the rim and dripped onto a flawlessly typed document Joan had spent the morning perfecting.

She cursed silently, then set her cup down and began picking the files up off the floor and stacking them on her desk. She would have to go through them eventually, so now was probably as good a time as any.

After two more cups of coffee and four files Chris opened one that she decided, after perusing it, had little to do with the case she was working on. But she continued to read. There was nothing unusual about the crime itself or the way in which the case had been handled. Still she continued to riffle through the pages in front of her.

Closing the file with a slam, Chris stared straight ahead, her breath heaving in ragged spurts. It couldn't be! There must be a mistake. Maybe there were two Warren J. Hamiltons.

She opened the file once again and reread the caption of the case. Warren was definitely connected with it. He was the attorney of record. But the strange thing was— the crazy, absurd, obviously mistaken thing was—that he was named as prosecuting attorney. Prosecutor? How could that be?

Chris quickly picked up the phone and dialed her boss. "Bill? Chris. Have you got a minute?"

"Not really, Chris. I was just heading out."

"Well, let me ask you a quick question then. Was Warren Hamilton a prosecutor at one time?"

"Yep, sure was. It was a hell of a long time ago though. Listen, is that it, Chris? I really have to go."

"With the D.A.'s office?" She couldn't yet grasp the reality of it.

"Yes. Bye, Chris. We'll talk later."

"Yeah . . . bye . . ." She spoke the last word into the air as she slowly lowered the phone to its cradle.

Warren a prosecutor. Incredible! But when? And why wasn't he any longer? Oh, don't be ridiculous, Chris. You know why. M-O-N-E-Y. Warren was obviously a man who valued money above principle, so why should he stick with the prosecuting game? He probably wasn't very good at it anyway . . . She continued to build the lies in her head, like laying one brick on top of another. To be a good prosecutor, you had to rely on principle. Money certainly wasn't the draw.

Chris dropped her face into her hands. Why, Warren? Why couldn't you have stuck it out? Why did you have to crave money so much? Why couldn't you be more like . . . me? Chris shook her head, knowing what a trumpeting, pompous snob she sounded like, even to herself.

God, but she missed him, and this seemed the only way to drive him from her mind. If she made him the embodiment of all evil, the worst blemish on the already blotched face of the American judicial system, she could forget him. She could believe all the lies she told herself about how her job in life was to slay the dragons of injustice, alone, without the help of any man. She had been right from the beginning. Warren had been wrong. She couldn't be a woman—the kind of woman a man expected her to be—and remain a good lawyer.

Chris sighed heavily as she stared out at the drizzling rain that stippled her dirty windowpane. She never had been a very good liar. And she would never, in a million years, forget Warren Hamilton.

"I just don't think we have enough evidence to convict, Bill."

"Okay." Bill accepted what she was saying, but still looked over the file in front of him to make sure. "We've got an eyewitness."

"But I'm not even sure I would want him to take the stand," Chris said.

"Hmm, well, let's see . . . we've got the police report and the arresting officer's testimony."

"An officer who, I might add, was placed on suspension a year ago for roughing up a suspect. I have gone over this quite a few times, Bill." Chris's voice had taken on a perturbed, snippy quality.

Bill looked up at her, staring directly, taking his time before he answered. "I'm sure you have, Chris. But I also happen to notice that the defense attorney in this case is Warren Hamilton."

Chris tried to control the flinch that had tightened the muscles in her body. "Meaning?"

"Chris, there's no need for you to go all stiff and indignant on me. I just want to make sure that personal relationships are not playing any part in your decision."

"There are no personal relationships involved here," Chris replied brusquely.

"Listen, Chris, when fireworks shoot off every time two people see each other the way they do with you and Warren, something personal is going on."

"Bill, we don't have a case. I am looking at this thing with total objectivity."

"Good." He nodded, still watching her closely. "Because if there is one thing in this country that deserves nothing less than total objectivity, it is the law. Fairness and equity for all parties involved." He looked back down at the file, flipping through the pages of notes, then closed the file and pushed it back over to Chris. "Notify Hamilton's firm that we're dropping the charges."

Chris nodded silently and picked up the file. She would have to ask Joan to call Warren and let him know. She couldn't yet face the task of actually speaking to him and hearing his voice on the other end of the line.

"Thanks, Bill." Chris opened the door of his office and started to step out into the hall.

"Oh, Chris, sorry I was too busy to answer your question about Warren the other day. You were wondering if he was a prosecutor at one time."

Her body tensed at the mere mention of his name again, and she couldn't release her hand from the doorknob.

"It was nothing." Her voice cracked and she had to clear her throat to continue. "Just something I ran across in the files." She had convinced herself that he was probably lousy as a prosecutor and had switched to the defense because of his lust for money and power. She had convinced herself, so she didn't want to discuss it with anyone and perhaps find out that her assumption was wrong.

"He was a hell of prosecutor," Bill mumbled under his breath as he pulled a stack of papers over in front of him and begin to leaf through them.

Chris was at once paralyzed. Her hand would not lift from the knob, her legs would not carry her through the doorway, her vocal chords would not allow her to speak. She turned back slowly, staring at Bill's head as he bowed over his work. "Good?" Her voice was a tiny squeak. "He was a good prosecutor?"

Bill glanced up, surprised to see her still standing there. He frowned as he tried to remember what they had been talking about, then nodded in recollection. "The best. In fact," he added, with no hint of malice, "if Warren had remained here, I probably wouldn't be in this job today."

170

"If he was so wonderful, why did he defect? Oh," she laughed unkindly, "stupid question, right? The money on the other side is quite a seductive draw."

Bill frowned as caught the venomous undertone. "Money wasn't the reason. Not that he hasn't enjoyed his stupendous success," he agreed. "Who wouldn't? But Warren certainly didn't . . . defect, as you put it. If anything, becoming a defense attorney was his form of self-preservation."

Now it was Chris's turn to frown. "What do you mean?"

"I mean, he was going to quit the law altogether." Bill shook his head gravely. "Now that would have been a tragedy."

"Why . . . why would he quit the law?" Chris stammered, sliding weakly into the chair in front of Bill's desk.

"He got the wrong man convicted. He was prosecuting in a case of grand larceny, and the defendant, a part-time clergyman, was sentenced to fifteen years. He was granted a retrial after four years, and the original conviction was vacated. It seems the state police in Alabama had arrested a man with the same modus operandi, and he made a full confession to the crime that took place here four years before."

"Oh, my God!" Chris closed her eyes tightly. "Four years." It was the one nightmare she—and probably every other prosecutor in the country with a conscience —had on a recurring basis, that she would one day convict the wrong person.

"Yeah, the man's wife left him, he lost his church, and most of his friends. It ruined his life. And, of course, Warren felt personally responsible."

"But he wasn't!"

"No, of course not," Bill agreed. "He was doing his job. He presented the evidence and it spoke for itself. Still . . . he took it really hard. But, after a while, he teamed up with Doddson and, as you are painfully aware, became one of the best damned defense attorneys in the state."

Chris was staring at the wall behind Bill, only half-listening to what he was saying. She was playing the scenes over in her mind. That night in his kitchen when she mentioned that he sounded more like a prosecutor than a defense attorney . . . the shutter that dropped over his expression . . . the day in her office when she sadistically congratulated him for defending a man who, six months later, killed a sixteen-year-old boy . . . the hurt in his eyes . . . the pain he must have been feeling. Now she understood why. Now she knew.

The only thing was—now it was too late. *A million years too late.*

CHAPTER 10

It was the envelope that caught her attention, the familiar return address in the upper left-hand corner. Doddson and Hamilton, Attorneys at Law. It was in the middle of the stack of mail that Joan had brought into Chris's office, already opened and stacked neatly with the envelopes paper-clipped on top of the correspondence.

Chris placed her palm flat against her stomach to still the painful trembling inside her. Was this the way it was always going to be? A simple letter, a phone call, a brief encounter in the clerk's office—would these trifling occurrences always shatter her the way they did now? Maybe there would come a time when it would no longer hurt so much, when she would not be seized with a shudder of longing at the mere mention of his name. Maybe, but she doubted that very seriously.

Trying to still her shaking fingers, she unclipped the envelope from the letter and began to read. With each expensively processed word she felt a stab of pain enter her body. He was cordially thanking her for dropping the charges against his client. Standard procedure. A polite gesture. Reciprocity. A courtesy between colleagues.

She held the letter next to her chest and, looking far into her mind, tried to read behind and between the lines. She imagined his voice as he recited the words into the Dictaphone. Were they just words to him, or had it been as difficult for him to say them in a detached tone as it was for her to listen to them? What was he feeling? Would he ever find it in his heart to forgive her?

She forced herself to continue reading the next paragraph. He was informing her that there would be a meeting with Co-Vestment on Thursday night. They were requesting her to attend, in the hope that they could finally reach a settlement of this matter.

Chris's thumb stroked across the bold, slanted signature. He had signed it Warren Hamilton, but his last name was scribbled so hastily that she couldn't help but feel that it had been written as a second thought.

She folded the letter neatly along its original creases, slipped it back into the envelope, and placed it in her purse. Thursday night . . . could she wait two days to see him again? What would his reaction be? What could she say to him to make him understand how sorry she was for the hurt she had caused him? Was "sorry" adequate?

They could have worked it out, she knew that now. They could have at least tried. He had been right; she was a very lonely woman. And it didn't have to be that way. She could have had a relationship with Warren and her career as well, but she had been too blind to see it. Now she had only her career. That and a very lonely existence.

Shaking her head at her own stupidity, she picked up the next letter on the stack of mail and began reading lethargically. Thursday night . . . would it ever come?

She set the brown leather briefcase down on the ground while she rubbed her hands together to remove the excess moisture. Never in her entire life had she been so nervous as she was at this moment. Breathing deeply to calm herself, she picked up the briefcase and kept walking toward the building. Stepping through the open glass doors and walking down the terrazzo hallway, she felt time slip away. It had been less than two months ago when she walked down this same corridor to meet with the officers of Co-Vestment and Warren Hamilton.

Less than two months, and yet it seemed like a lifetime ago. She was a completely different person now, and she had passed through an eternity of unhappiness since that last meeting.

Pushing open the wooden doors to the office, Chris was greeted by the president, vice-president, and a secretary.

"Mr. Hamilton should be along any minute," the president explained as he led them into the conference room. Their attitude toward Chris was polite and reserved, but she sensed that they had considerably softened their belligerent stance on the Willow Towers issue.

When they were all seated around the conference table, the secretary hurried through the door to get them cups of coffee. When the door opened again,

Chris automatically turned to reach for her cup from the secretary.

Time froze in a capsulated eternity as Warren stepped into the room. Their eyes locked in a greeting that startled them both with its ability to virtually stop time and to seal them both inside their self-enclosed private universe.

Only the two of them were aware that the moment had lasted forever. The others in the room were unaware that anything out of the ordinary had happened. As Warren took his seat the secretary finally returned with the cups of coffee and, efficiency being her forte, set an extra one down in front of him.

They were seated across from one another, and Chris had to call upon all the reserves of her conscious mind to keep from constantly staring at him. But in that brief moment when she had watched him walk through the door, every detail of his appearance had imprinted itself upon her mind.

He was dressed in a dark pinstripe suit, a crisp white shirt with a navy-and-burgundy silk tie gracing his magnificent chest. In a fit of rebellious craving she mentally peeled the jacket from his arms, slowly and tortuously. Her fingers loosened the tie, tugged it around the collar of his shirt, and tossed it across the room. Then, in one swift movement, her hands raked down the front of his shirt, wrenching it open and sending the buttons flying through the air. She could touch his chest, she could run her hands across the warm flesh of his body.

Involuntarily her eyes lifted to his face, and she saw in his expression that he had detected the desire she felt for him in the moist depths of her gray eyes.

"Now." The president officiously opened his brief-case and pulled a stack of papers from inside. "Let's get started."

Chris swallowed in an effort to rid her throat and chest of the constricting tightness. She also opened her briefcase and pulled out a file full of notes and contracts, a yellow legal pad, and a pen.

"Ms. Davis, since our last meeting, we have had a new survey done on the property and"—the president cleared his throat—"as you already knew, it appears that the original survey was in error. It seems that Mr. Palmer, a tenant in Willow Towers, owns a substantial portion of the lot on which the building stands. Now, we have consulted with our attorney, Mr. Hamilton." He nodded in Warren's direction. "And we have been advised by him on the best course of action to take."

Chris held her breath, hoping that she had done her homework well enough that there were no holes that the company would be allowed to slip through. She and Clifford had talked for long hours about what he wanted for his property and about the possibility that Co-Vestment would find another way around this obstacle. She glanced surreptitiously at Warren and noticed that he was watching her steadily. Her breath caught and held as she felt the riveting stare drill into the mask of reserve she was wearing.

"Warren, would you like to take it from here?" the president asked.

"All right." Warren tore his gaze away from Chris, glancing down at the papers in front of him. Chris couldn't control the jolt of electricity that shot through her body when his voice first caressed her name. "The way we understand it, Ms. Davis, Clifford Palmer is willing to sell his interest in the property and the lot next door for one hundred thousand dollars. Is that correct?" He looked directly at her, and she realized in that moment that this encounter was as painful for him as it was for her. His face was drawn, and the brown of his eyes had dulled to the color of dry wood.

"That's correct, but there are other conditions, of course."

"We're aware of that, Ms. Davis," The vice-president couldn't hide the snide tone that curled around his tongue.

Warren quickly inserted a conciliatory remark. "I have the contract that Ms. Davis sent to our office with a list of conditions, and I thought maybe we could go over them together."

Chris switched her gaze away from the arrogant vice-president and back to Warren. A sense of pride washed through her as she listened to his reasonable tone, his ability to carry on professionally even under the most trying circumstances.

She consulted the contract in front of her, and agreed that he should read them aloud.

" 'Witnesseth,' " Warren began, "that Seller, Clifford T. Palmer, for the considerations hereinafter mentioned, does grant, convey, etc., etc. the property hereinafter described: being all that land situated in the southwest quarter of the northwest quarter of Section 30 herein described in the plat of Tulsa County . . . and so on and so forth.' We all know what land where talking about, don't we?" Warren smiled and was answered with a few soft chuckles.

" 'To be paid unto Seller the sum of twenty-five thousand dollars. Seller will transfer said parcel of land if and only if, first, Buyer is also willing to purchase the adjacent lot' . . . and I will omit the legal description, here. If anyone is interested, he can read it on his own copy of the contract . . . 'for the sum of seventy-five thousand dollars.' " He looked at Chris. "Are these conditions correct so far?"

"Yes," Chris nodded.

"Okay. Second, as we understand it, 'Mr. Palmer requires that the Owner, Co-Vestment Incorporated, allow the thirty-five undersigned tenants, hereinafter referred to as the Tenants, to remain at Willow Towers under the terms of all extant leases with said tenants. Furthermore, the Tenants shall not, on this date or on any future date, be persecuted, harassed, or inconvenienced in any manner calculated to intimidate or to induce the Tenants to vacate the premises currently occupied by them.' "

"My God!" the vice-president exploded. "Is this clause really necessary? I mean after all . . ."

"I think Ms. Davis is just trying to cover all angles, gentlemen," Warren answered calmly. "I think the clause should stay as is."

Chris looked at Warren and a smile hovered around her mouth.

"Now," he continued in his professional tone, "if Ms. Davis will permit, we have a few conditions of our own that we would like to discuss with her."

"Of course," she answered in the same tone he was using, holding back the deep, emotional feelings she had for him.

"Co-Vestment agrees to purchase the above described property, including the vacant lot adjacent to the Willow Towers apartment complex for the price of one hundred thousand dollars. Co-Vestment also agrees to allow the thirty-five tenants named in the contract to remain at Willow Towers at the same monthly rental, plus a ten percent increase at the end of every two-year period; the first period shall end two years from the signing of said contract.

"However, monthly payments shall be divided into principal, interest, and escrow accounts and shall be applied toward the purchase of individual units. If Tenants, thereafter to be called Purchasers, wish to vacate the premises, they are responsible for the sale of their individual units."

Warren looked up at Chris, his face completely void of expression. But she noticed the tightly held muscles in his jaws as he waited for her reply.

She was silent for several moments. She wasn't really surprised that they had their own conditions. In fact, she had expected them to ask for more than the ones Warren just read. How hard had he pushed Co-Vestment to agree to this contract? Had he tried after all to make this fair to the tenants of Willow Towers?

She was looking at him and the questioning wonder blazed from the depths of her eyes. Forcibly tearing her gaze away from him, she glanced around the table at the officers waiting for her reply. Slowly she nodded.

"I believe we can live with these conditions, gentlemen. My secretary will type up the new contracts tomorrow. She has been kind enough to help with this project on her own time, and I know she will be as relieved as I'm sure we all are that an agreement has been reached." Chris smiled for the first time tonight, and the president of the company reached across the table to shake her hand.

Tentatively and awkwardly Chris and Warren extended their hands across the table to shake on the deal. When her hand met his, she felt an indescribable heat filter into her bloodstream and along the tattered nerve endings of her body. She wanted to clench his hand tightly, to never let go, to pull every particle of strength from his body, absorbing it through her skin where it would strengthen her own body. She wanted him—however she could have him, she wanted him.

When their hands were withdrawn, an anticlimactic gloom settled over her. The problem was solved with Co-Vestment, and other than for the formal signing of the contract, she would not be meeting with Warren about it again.

As she pulled her mouth into a now fraudulent smile, she made her polite good-byes and left the office. Standing outside in the hallway, she hesitated. Perhaps she should wait for Warren, try to explain how sorry she was for the hurt she must have caused him. But no, he probably wouldn't want to talk to her anyway. He might even come out with the Co-Vestment people. How embarrassing would it be for her to be standing here waiting for him!

But then, did she really care if she was embarrassed or not? Wasn't the fact that she apologized to him the only important thing? It was time to stop worrying about herself; she had done that for too long—and with disastrous consequences.

When the double wooden doors opened, Chris pressed her back more tightly against the wall, trying to blend into the walnut paneling.

He stepped through the opening, alone, and started to walk toward the front entrance. But something caught his eye, a flash of color, perhaps a flickering movement. He turned and faced Chris, his expression hidden from her by the dark shadows of the hallway.

Chris stepped away from the wall and stood in front of him. Even from this close she could tell his expression was being carefully guarded. Nothing, no hint of forgiveness or affection, was revealed in the rigid set of his mouth and jaw or in the flat color of his eyes.

The awkward moments of silence circled and played around them like a death knell. She had to say something. She had to prove that what she felt for him was still alive. Chris moistened her lips with her tongue and opened her mouth to speak. Several long seconds elapsed before the words issued forth.

"Warren . . . I know you'll probably never forgive me for my behavior . . . You probably don't want to even waste your time listening to me . . . but I have to tell you. I am so sorry for what I said that day in my office . . . about Fred Zimmerman . . . about you." She cleared her throat as a lump of tears worked its way upward. She blinked a few times to keep it at bay. "I was upset because I thought you had said things about me at your office that were . . . I made the mistake of assuming that you had used me. It was childish of me and . . . wrong."

The tears were pushing against her lower lid and she knew she could no longer restrain them. She had to leave, had to get away from him before she made a blubbering fool of herself. "You are the . . ." She wiped at the drops falling on her cheeks and cleared her throat again. "You're the best friend I've ever had, Warren. I just want you to know that." She turned and began walking quickly toward the exit before the sobs broke loose from her throat.

"Christine?" The sound skimmed along the terrazzo tile, reverberating through her mind and body. The rich sound of her name alone was the most beautiful sound she had ever heard. An electrical tremor moved in waves through her system, rippling, jolting the very core of her being.

She turned slowly and watched him walk toward her, his eyes now soft with the polished glow she had come to love so much. "Christine," he breathed again in wonderment. His hand reached up and touched her cheek, brushing lightly at a tear that still remained. "I've missed you."

"Oh, God, Warren." Chris's fingers clutched his hand where it still rested on her cheek. "I'm so sorry! I've been so foolish! So childish! So . . ."

"Enough, Christine," Warren whispered as he reached around her with his left arm, pulling her close to him. "We've both made mistakes. Maybe I rushed you too much. I wasn't honest enough with you about my past mistakes. There are things I haven't told you . . ."

"About being a prosecutor?"

He glanced uneasily at her. "Yes."

"I know all about it, Warren. I think I can understand how deeply it affected you."

"It's been hard for me, Christine."

"I know it has." She flattened a palm against his chest.

"No . . . no you don't. I hope to hell you never know. But, I'm at least glad it's out in the open between us. I wanted to tell you, but . . . did Bill tell you?"

"Yes."

Warren nodded. "He's been a good friend over the years."

"I want to be your friend too, Warren."

He looked down at her upturned face, his eyes traveling from her hair to her eyes to her mouth. "And what else?" he smiled easily, but Chris sensed the importance of the question—and her answer—to him.

"I want to be everything to you, Warren. Everything that you need and want. I know now that the woman in me really does want to be free. And, I want to share that part of me with you. I've made us waste so much time when we could have been together."

Warren's eyes closed as he pulled her head against his chest, his mouth brushing the top of her scalp and his arms holding her tightly, as if he were trying to absorb her essence into his own body.

After a long moment Chris laughed nervously. "What are we going to tell the Co-Vestment crew if they come out here and catch us?"

"We'll tell them we're sealing the contract, of course."

"I thought we did that with a handshake," she tilted her head back to look up at him.

"Oh, but this way is much . . . much more binding." His head lowered and his mouth covered hers in a gentle but solemn assurance of his love for her. She could feel the acceleration of his heart next to hers every second their mouths remained in contact.

When he finally released her, his eyes had warmed to a deep brown glow and his hands caressed her arms with barely suppressed need.

He reached up and touched the frame of her glasses.

184

"I thought you were supposed to have your contacts by now."

Chris looked down self-consciously. "I do have them, but . . . I hate them. They hurt, and they're a pain in the neck to keep clean."

"Good." He laughed, which made her glance up with a start. "I want you just the way you are. The way you were when I first saw you tripping over tables."

"Sadistic devil." She grinned. "Well, do you think we should get out of here before the president of Co-Vestment catches us?"

"Yes, and I have something for you, Christine. It's out at the house."

She looked surprised, but said nothing.

"It's something I've wanted to show you for . . . well, for a while. I was beginning to wonder if I was ever going to get the chance."

"What on earth is it, Warren?" She was truly perplexed, but the feeling of excitement that was bubbling upward made it hard to keep from fidgeting like a little kid at Christmas.

"You have to come to the house to see it." He winked slyly, then looked at her gravely. "Do you want to come now?"

Chris didn't miss the hopeful tone in his voice and look of the anticipation that flickered nervously across his eyes. "Yes, I want to come now."

Sighing with relief, Warren led her to the parking lot where they each got into their own cars, he into his red Thunderbird and she into a used Chevrolet that, according to the salesman, had been a real steal.

She followed him, and he always made sure that he didn't leave her behind at a traffic light. Her thoughts and her heart were racing a mile a minute all the way to his house. She was going to Warren's house! He had if not forgotten, at least forgiven her for her insensitive behavior toward him. He loved her, and she loved him!

The first thing Chris noticed as they pulled down the dark, winding road to his house, was a pile of gray junk sitting in the driveway. The closer they came, the more it began to take shape. It was obviously metal, but what on earth . . .

By the time she had parked her car and stepped out onto the driveway, her mind had absorbed what he had waiting for her. She couldn't believe it! He had done that for her?

"I know it doesn't look like much right now, Christine," he hurried to reassure her. "But half the fun of owning one of these old . . . sorry, classic cars is in fixing them up."

Chris walked around the wrecked MGA that sat lopsided in the driveway, and she knew in that moment that she loved Warren more than anyone or anything in the whole world.

"You found this car for me?" Her voice was incredulous.

"Yes, in Bartlesville. The day I went over to take depositions and you . . . were having lunch with Ben."

She stared at him in amazement. The day she had cursed him up and down for what she supposed he had done to her was the day he spent selflessly searching through junkyards for a car to replace the one she had lost in Oklahoma City.

"Warren, I don't know what to say." She walked over to him and placed her hand on the front of his shirt, gazing up at him with love.

He shrugged, a little embarrassed by his own magnanimity. "Just say you'll fix it up and get it out of the middle of the driveway." He laughed, reaching around her waist with his arms to keep her from escaping.

"Tell me where to begin," she smiled coquettishly, "and I'll start right now."

"First things first." His grasped a handful of her hair, and his mouth swooped down to take possession of hers.

Throwing her arms around his neck, he pulled her into a tight embrace, lifting her off the ground while he wrapped her in a bear hug.

When they pulled their heads back to look at each other, their eyes were blazing with the love and the need that filled them both.

"Before we go in the house—" Warren stopped for a moment and stared at her, simply stared at the loveliness of her face as she looked up at him. "I want you to know, Christine, that I'm not interested in having an affair with you. I mean, that's just not enough for me."

She watched him closely, afraid to even speculate on the words he would use next, holding in her breath in hopes that they would be the ones she wanted to hear most.

He cleared his throat a little awkwardly. "Would you . . . that is, will you marry me, Christine?"

The breath she had been holding in spilled into the night and wrapped around them in a sigh of yes, yes, yes.

Pulling back into a long, tender embrace, Chris pressed her mouth into Warren's neck. "I would love to marry you, Warren. I don't want to live another day without you."

"Then don't," he breathed huskily against her temple. "Don't." With that, he picked her up in his arms and carried her into the house and directly into his bedroom.

Laying her down gently across the bedspread, he sat down beside her and for several minutes, they simply gazed at each other in fascination. It was like a dream, Chris knew. Fairytales like this didn't happen in real life; not to people like her anyway. But Warren had asked her to marry him. He loved her. He wanted her.

Her hand reached up to stroke his jaw, and the moment of stunned silence was gone. Warren bent over, pressing his lips against her neck, trailing his tongue along the silken column of her throat, nibbling, tasting, moving upward to her ear and temple.

She reached with both hands to pull him down to her, but his shoulders stiffened. "No," he whispered.

"Warren?"

"No." He placed a gentle finger against her lips. "Not yet." He stood up and slowly began removing his coat and tie. Chris leaned up on her elbows, her chest rising and falling in rapid succession as she watched him slowly peeling the shirt and trousers from his body. When he was no longer clothed, she reached for him, but he drew her arms back gently to the sides of her head.

His fingers, deliberately slow, unfastened the buttons on the front of her dress, easing it off her shoulders and pulling it down over her body until it too was draped across the chair. The thought of just her clothes mingled so intimately with his sent a thrill of anticipation through her bloodstream.

Once again she reached for him, but he slowly shook

188

his head. With her arms still resting above her head, he slowly trailed his fingers down her body, from the top of her head to the tips of her toes—silken strokes that teased and tantalized her nerve endings until she felt that they would ignite from the scorching touch of his hands.

Her blood was pounding at all of her pulse points, and she felt the devouring spike of his gaze along every angle and curve of her body.

His hand moved between her thighs and his fingers enticed her, holding her at bay until she was almost consumed by the fire within.

When she tried to pull him down on top of her, he dropped down beside her, propped up on one elbow. Holding her hands above her head, his lips moved onto her breasts, and she arched her back as he drew her flesh into his mouth. Ever so slowly he dropped gentle kisses over her abdomen, then lowered his head between her thighs.

Chris grasped his head in her hands, grabbing thick strands of his hair with urgent fingers, her moans raking along his flesh as sensually as her fingernails. "Warren, please!"

He lifted his head to watch the passion radiating from her eyes. He raised up and moved his weight between her legs, lowering his mouth toward hers with infinite patience. "Yes," he breathed huskily. "Now."

He moved into her, stroking, pulsating, and the glory of their love expanded with the universe into the boundless arms of space, a pocket of sweet oblivion that cradled them in timeless splendor.

Later, when they were folded within each other's arms, they breathed exhausted but exhilarated sighs, hands still stroking chests or thighs, lips pressing light kisses against a shoulder or a cheek. It was even longer still before either of them could speak.

"I'm convinced that we can make this work, Warren. I know there will be many a time when we don't agree on issues, but—"

"But our marriage will never be dull." He teased her ear with his lips. "Besides, we're both fighting for the same thing, you know . . . equal justice under the law. Between the two of us we've got the entire spectrum covered."

"Warren?" Chris's voice was soft and low in the sultry air of the bedroom. "Why did Co-Vestment . . . you . . . give so much on the Willow Towers contract?"

"I was only trying to be fair."

"You were more than fair, Warren, and you know it. Willow Towers definitely came out ahead."

"You deserved to, Chris." He kissed her temple and lightly brushed a strand of damp hair away from her face. "You did your homework, you found the flaw in the survey and . . . and you cared so much for those people. It was only right that the settlement was in your favor."

She lifted up on her elbow, draping her body over his side and thigh. "I love you, Warren. I've been wrong about so many things. I was never the one with the principles; it is you who are the noblest, the most decent, and the most honest person I have ever known."

"I'm just a man, Chris." Warren's hand stroked along her hip and thigh, but he was looking directly at Chris, wanting her to understand what his life was all about. He didn't want there to be any disappointments later. "I make mistakes. I plod along like the rest of humanity and hope that my good deeds outweigh the bad ones. But, I can never be sure. I'm just a man."

Chris feigned surprise and smiled crookedly. "And all along I thought you were some sort of deity. Well." She shrugged. "I've been warned. I guess I'll just have to take you as you are. *Caveat emptor* and all that."

He chuckled deep within his throat as his eyes roamed possessively down her face and onto her breasts. "And pray tell, counselor, what will you do with me after you have me?" He tightened his hold around her waist, pulling her up between the spread of his thighs.

She closed her eyes briefly as the heat between their flesh spread like wine through her bloodstream. "I will do what any smart consumer does . . ." Her mouth and tongue moved down across his chest, returning slowly up his neck and over his chin, where she then breathed softly and seductively into his waiting mouth. "I will consume you." *Forever.*

LOOK FOR NEXT MONTH'S
CANDLELIGHT ECSTASY ROMANCE®